Gold Magic

Bruce Davis

Brick Cave Media
brickcavebooks.com

Gold Magic

Cover Illustration Artist: Thitipon Decruen
www.xric7.com

Brick Cave Media
brickcavebooks.com
2020

To

Russell and Matthew,

for keeping life exciting and inspiring.

Also by Bruce Davis

Available from Brick Cave Books

MAGIC LAW SERIES
Platinum Magic

THE PROFIT LOGS
GlowGems for Profit
Thieves Profit

GOLD MAGIC

BRUCE DAVIS

Brick Cave Media
brickcavebooks.com

CHAPTER ONE

Simon Buckley drove the high-speed lane of the eastbound W205 at well above the legal limit. His black Oxley Tornado had enough power in the Air spell charging its cinnabar impregnated frame to maintain the speed, and the King's Peacekeeper shield on the front bumper ensured that none of the local authorities along the highway would stop him. At just past the fourth hour of the day, there was hardly any other traffic anyway.

Just as Simon passed over the Finnegan Estuary on the Prince Henrik Bridge and entered the city of Cymbeline, the summoning tone on his handheld magic mirror rang. He swiped a hand across its surface and glanced down as Haldron Stonebender's bearded face swam into view.

Hal's expression was grim. "Where are you, lad?" he asked, his Dwarfish burr more pronounced than usual.

"Just crossed the Prince Henrik, Hal," said Simon. "What's all this about?"

"Best not to talk on the mirror," Hal answered. "Don't bother going home or to the House. Have you got your badge and sidearm?"

"Of course," said Simon.

"Good. Get off the 205 at Canal Street and head north. Corner of Canal and Knacker. Now that you're close, I'll be calling the rest of the team. You're the Ranking Keeper, so we won't have much official steel until you get here."

"Not Lily's Place again," groaned Simon.

"No, but the lot right next to it. And she is the president of the Hollows Business Guild. She's the reason our team caught this cave-in of a case. I think she likes you."

"How bad is it?"

"Bad," Hal said. "Just get down here."

Ten minutes later, Simon pulled up behind a black Keeper sled with its green and orange warning lights still flashing. He canceled the Air spell and his Oxley settled to the pavement. He picked up the holster from the passenger side seat, slid out the Czech and Hawley spring powered needler, and checked his weapon automatically. The Earth spell that activated the spring was fully charged and the sixteen-round magazine held standard sleeper darts. He clipped the holster to his right hip.

Hal heaved himself off of the bumper of a Keeper sled and approached as Simon climbed out onto the sidewalk.

"Nice slide," said Hal.

"Don't start, Hal," said Simon. "Sylvie gave me enough grief when she first saw it. She thinks it's too expensive and that I bought it just so I could get to the Borderlands faster."

"And she's wrong about that?"

"Shut up, Hal."

The Dwarf just laughed at him and Simon had to smile.

"What was so damned important that I had to cut my leave short?" Simon asked.

"Come and see," said Hal, his face turning grim.

As they walked toward the bright work lights in the vacant lot ahead, Hal spoke quickly. "The Civil Enforcement squad caught the first squawk and sent a couple of sleds. They called in the forensics team. Kyle Evarts had the night duty, and I guess things were slow because he decided to come himself. He's the one who listened to Lily and summoned us, or summoned me rather. I had a look and decided to interrupt your time with Sylvie."

They reached the focus of all the attention. Simon flashed his badge and a Patrol Agent lifted the orange crime scene rope for him. At first, all he could see was a half dozen Crime Scene Analysis mages clustered around a tarp laid out on the ground. Only when he got closer did he make out the four pairs of small bare feet.

Dear Mother, they're children. Who would do this to children?

They were indeed Orc children, pitifully small and thin, clad in identical blue smocks with bare feet and arms. They lay in a neat row, their hands almost touching. Their eyes were closed and their faces looked peaceful. He might have thought they were sleeping if not for the bloodless pallor of their skin and the wide slash wounds across their throats.

Simon knelt beside the nearest child, a girl he noted, and checked her wrists. The marks were subtle but distinct. She had been bound with some sort of wide restraint, maybe padded with soft cloth. For an instant, his mind flashed back to another cold night, kneeling beside the body of his father, clutching the man's lifeless hand in a mute appeal for rescue.

Children. They're not but children. He controlled a sudden surge of revulsion and anger that threatened to take his breath away. He looked up at Hal. "Blood Magic," he said.

Hal nodded.

"Lily saw it right away but our mates in the Civil squad didn't heed her. Evarts, though, he listened, and when he saw the wounds and the restraint marks, summoned me."

"Who's the scene commander?"

Hal made a sour face. "Frank Killian."

"So he kept his badge," said Simon with a shake of his head.

"After a fashion." Hal grimaced. "He rolled over on Gulbrandsen in a deal with the King's Prosecutor. Got broken from Sergeant to Senior Patrol Agent and transferred to the Civil squad, but he's still a Keeper."

A few months earlier, Simon and his team had exposed a conspiracy involving his immediate superior, a Peacekeeper Lieutenant named Gulbrandsen, and an Undersecretary from the Elf homeland, the Gray Havens. The two had helped supply Azeri terrorists with Fire grenades in the hopes of inciting a war between the Commonwealth and the Azeri Empire. The Havens would have taken advantage of a weakening of the Commonwealth economy, and Gulbrandsen hoped to get rich from war profiteering. Gulbrandsen had been Killian's patron. Then Sergeant Killian with the Magic Enforcement Squad hadn't known precisely what his boss was doing but had concealed evidence that might have implicated the Havens in the plot.

Simon rose to his feet. "Lets go find him," he said with a frown.

Hal pointed toward the back entrance to the squat building next to the lot. A clot of uniformed Patrol Agents milled about there as if trying to work themselves into some sort of order.

As he drew closer, Simon could hear a shrill voice shouting in a mixture of Common Speech and Azeri. Before he could make sense of the words, two of the uniformed Keepers were thrust bodily aside. Lily Ponsaka burst from the group and stormed toward Simon.

She was a short, broad, Orc woman, with the dark skin and almond shaped eyes of the Southron Azeri race. Her multicolored skirts, green vest, and short-sleeved blouse were inadequate protection from the cold air, but she showed no signs of feeling it. The Fish Clan tattoos that wound around her thick forearms seemed to bulge and flex as she pushed her way through the small crowd.

"What in the hells took you so long, Simon Buckley?" She shook her forefinger at him. "I've been telling that fool Killian that this was Blood magic for the past four hours."

"I'm here now, Lily," Simon said calmly. He inclined his head toward Hal. "You know Hal Stonebender. You can thank him for calling me away from my leave to rush back here and talk to you." Lily reluctantly nodded in Hal's direction but did not take her eyes off of Simon.

"Now, where is SP Killian?" Simon asked.

"Back there with the rest of the Bluebellies," Lily jerked a thumb over her shoulder. "Drinking my coffee and making a show of being tough and in charge." She sighed. "Oh, he's not a bad sort for a Keeper. And the patrols have been more regular since he took charge of this beat, but he's put this down as some sort of gang revenge killing. I'm no shaman, but I know Blood magic when I see it. That's why I've been screaming for you."

They had been working their way back toward the rear entrance to Lily's Place, a combination tavern, rooming house and unofficial community center that had become a focal point for Orc activism in the Hollows.

Francis Killian leaned against the doorframe, sipping from a mug and quietly speaking to one of his Patrol Keepers. He saw Simon and stiffened.

"How are you, Frank?" Simon extended his hand.

Killian took it and shook, rather stiffly. "Getting by, Sergeant Buckley," he said, meeting Simon's eye.

"What's the situation?"

"I suppose you've seen the bodies?" When Simon said nothing, he went on. "One of Mistress Ponsaka's kitchen maids found them when she came out here to dump the scraps. The Patrol Unit that responded to the summoning realized it wasn't just another random killing and called for backup. They obviously weren't killed here and the positioning of the bodies shows this wasn't just a random dump site. This lot was chosen for a reason. I'm thinking it's the Knacker Street Loblollies that dumped them there. There's been bad blood between them and the Canal Street Scalpers. And this is the edge of Scalper territory."

"My place is Neutral Ground," said Lily. "Everybody knows that."

Killian shrugged. "Maybe, maybe not. Maybe somebody is sending a message to the Scalpers to back off of the jolt trade on the other side of Knacker. Some of their dealers have been selling as far west as the Old Wall."

Simon held up a hand to silence Lily when she opened her mouth to shout at Killian. "I agree with you about the bodies being moved and this being no random dump site. I'm not so sure about the Loblolly connection, though." Killian started to speak, but Simon continued before he could say anything. "It's an interesting idea, Frank. Probably worth pursuing. But for now, Magic Enforcement will be taking charge. Both Kyle Evarts and I agree that this looks like a Blood Magic sacrifice. I don't know which spell or curse, but all Blood magic involving sentient beings is proscribed by the Accords. I'll need to detail a couple of your people for a crime scene canvass until the rest of my team gets here."

Killian frowned. "Is that an order, Sergeant?"

"It's a request, Frank. But I'll make it an order if that's what you want."

They regarded one another for a long moment, Killian glaring and Simon returning his look, remaining calm. Simon was the ranking Keeper on scene; Killian had no choice but to comply, and they both knew it.

After a second, Killian looked away and grunted acquiescence. "I'll let you have Jerrill and Steelhelm. They took the initial call and should be allowed to see it through." He pointed a finger at Simon. "You keep me in the circle.

Agreed?"

"As you say, Frank," replied Simon.

Killian turned and handed his mug to Lily. "Thanks for the coffee, Mistress Ponsaka. I'll have my boys cleared out of here shortly. Send the bill for anything they ate or drank to Wycliffe House, my name on it. I'll see that you're paid."

Lily accepted the mug. "Only fair. I'll send it along."

Killian sketched a salute toward Simon and strode away shouting orders to his team.

"He's not a bad sort," Lily repeated to no one in particular. "Just thick as swamp mud."

"Why don't you tell me what you know about these children, Lily," Simon placed a hand on the doorframe and leaned close so only Lily could hear him.

Lily looked at him sharply. "Me? Why would I know anything about a bunch of throwaway kids? It's enough that I can recognize a Blood sacrifice and do your lot's work for you. What more do you want from me?"

Simon shook his head. "And how do you know they're throwaways?"

Lily looked away and didn't speak for a long second. "One of the girls used to come by the back door and ask for work in exchange for a meal. I'd have her sweep the porch, and give her enough food for a couple of days. I think she hid out in one of the boathouses just south of here."

"And the others?"

"I saw one of the boys on the street now and again, always by himself. Figured he was one of them. The other two, I never saw before."

"Any chance one of the other shopkeepers on Canal might know who they were?" Simon asked.

Lily shrugged. "Maybe, if they gave it any thought. Throwaways, nobody notices. When was the last time one of Frank Killian's lads paid any attention to a throwaway kid down here in the Hollows?"

Life could be hard for Orcs, Simon reflected, even in

modern Cymbeline. Orc families struggled more than most. Sometimes, when the money ran out, or the promises smelted down to nothing but dross, hope died. Desperate parents would turn out the oldest or the most promising child to make their own way in order to have enough to feed the rest. Sometimes it worked out. It had been that way with Lily herself. But sometimes, children were simply abandoned. Whole families packed up and moved, leaving one or more children behind to fend for themselves. Throwaways.

Simon had been fortunate enough to find a good foster family after he had been orphaned when an Azeri loan leech had killed his father. He glanced over at Hal and smiled to himself. He looked back at Lily who was watching him warily.

"So at least two of the kids were from the Hollows," he said. "What do you hear in the tavern, Lily? Any rumors of missing children, or wild tales of Blood sacrifices?"

Lily scratched her chin in thought "Nothing. Oh, there's the usual gruesome stories of headless bodies in the canals and strange monsters roaming the alleys at night, snatching babies from their cribs, but those are old country tales. Most of them are harmless."

Simon looked across the lot to where the CSA team was beginning to remove the four small bodies. *Maybe not so harmless.*

"Not lately," said Hal. "He's left the Darrowdowns, you know. His sister told me he moved out a week ago. He's got himself a small flat, up in West Wray, not far from Reba and the kids."

"Is Reba all good with that?" asked Simon.

Hal shrugged. "Ham was killed in the line of duty, so she's got his pension and death benefit, but with three kids, it's still a hard rock for her to move. Jack's been helping out when she'll let him. It's part of paying *were geld,* lad. Something Jack has to do."

Simon smiled. He'd been orphaned at ten and Hal had taken him in as a foster son after that. Despite being raised in a Dwarfish household, there were still things about the culture that Simon didn't fully understand.

"As long as he shows up and does his job, it's all good as far as the Force is concerned," said Simon. "But Jack's a friend, and a teammate. We're all worried about him."

"All?"

"Rein in, Hal. Kermal may not have known Ham, but he can tell something is off with the rest of us and that it centers on Jack. It's hard enough being the new guy."

"And did you never consider, lad, how Jack might feel about an Orc replacing Hamish McPhee?" asked Hal.

"No, I didn't," said Simon, his voice now flat and cold. In truth he had considered it. He knew how he felt about it; about the hole that Ham's death had left that Brackenville could never fill. *Given time, Kermal will make his own mark on the team. But by the gods, I can't let personal feelings get in the way of this team doing its job.* "Neither should you, Hal. He took the Kings shilling, and the Oath, just like the rest of us. He's a Peacekeeper, no different from you and Jack. And as long as he does his job and watches my back, I don't care where he comes from or who his parents were. If that's not good enough for you or for Jack, you can put in for a transfer to another team any time."

And you're so good at suppressing feelings, right?

Hal's face reddened, and Simon feared for a moment that he'd pushed him too far. But the old Dwarf swallowed hard, making a sour face as if he'd just eaten something bitter, before taking a deep breath and visibly calming himself. He looked away from Simon, his face grim. "Is that any way to talk to your foster father?" he asked.

Simon smiled. "It is if my foster father is being an ass."

Hal sighed heavily before looking back at Simon, a faint smile on his face. "Aye, I suppose you're right. But change is a hard thing." The smile broadened. "Don't worry, lad. I'll try harder and I'll see to it that Jack does too."

"All good then." Simon returned the smile. Can you think of anything I missed?"

"Lily knows more than she's saying," said Hal. "Now's not the time to push her, but I'm thinking another talk with her would be a good idea."

"Do you still have any contacts down here in the Hollows?"

Hal grew thoughtful. "Snick hasn't said much of late. He's lying low; afraid the Azeris will connect him to our operation from a few months ago. I can press him, but he like as not won't have much for us."

"No," Simon shook his head. "He's too valuable over the long term to risk scaring him off."

"There are a few other tunnel crawlers I can squeeze. The Stone feels rotten on this one. Blood magic is dark enough business when it's done with pigs and chickens. Gods know I've got no love for Orcs, but the Seven Hells aren't deep enough for anyone who'd kill a child."

Simon trusted Hal's Stone sense, but didn't need it to know that these poor children weren't the end of this case. The blue smocks, the similarities in age, the evident care with which they were laid out, even the fact that there were two of each sex, all implied ritual and purpose. Whoever had done this had a dark end in mind, and wasn't going to stop at these four killings.

CHAPTER THREE

Simon stayed on the scene until the last of the bodies was loaded into the morgue sledge. Jack and the Civil Patrol agents had made a good start on the neighborhood canvass. Simon doubted they would learn much. Orcs down in the Hollows didn't talk to Peacekeepers willingly. Still, it was good procedure and Simon would have felt remiss if he hadn't ordered it.

Kermal departed after a brief conversation with Lily. Simon had higher hopes for his efforts. Despite wearing the dark blue uniform of the King's Peacekeepers, Brackenville was obviously at least half Orc. He spoke fluent Azeri and had shown before today that he could be discreet. He might persuade other Orcs to talk to him, especially if missing children were involved.

Simon waved a hand to Hal, indicating he should take charge and walked slowly back to his Oxley. He was groggy from lack of sleep, having driven through most of the night to get to Cymbeline after Hal's summons.

He leaned against the sled looking up. The early spring sky was cold and cloudless, lit only by the stars. Simon had appreciated the sight hours earlier, snuggled next to Sylvie Graystorm in a warm bed. They had sipped mulled wine while gazing out the window of the small but very private inn midway between Cymbeline and the Borderlands of the Gray Havens where Sylvie was stationed. The innkeeper had come to know them and always reserved the same room on the upper floor for them when they met there. The big skylight over the double bed offered spectacular stargazing. From here in the heart of the Orc slums, the stars had little of the same luster. He climbed into the sled with a sigh and activated the Air spell.

Under the Commonwealth Accords, all races were equal; Humans, Dwarves, Elves, Orcs, and even those few Halflings that had survived the Wars of the Races that had destroyed the old Magisterium. All were recognized to have natural rights to life, property, freedom from slavery, and equal treatment under the Kings law. In practice it had taken many years before all of the laws restricting Orc property ownership outside of the Reservations set aside for them had been repealed. Even now, few Orcs lived anywhere but in the neighborhoods that had once been their only legal residences. The Hollows harbored the Commonwealth's largest concentration of Orcs outside of the Southern Reservation, many of them immigrants and refugees from the Azeri Empire.

He pulled the sled away from the curb and drove slowly down Canal toward Tanner Street. Canal Street followed one of the artificial waterways from which it took its name. Hundreds of canals had been dug over the course of the city's history connecting the wide Finnegan River to the interior countryside as well as to the industrial and commercial centers of Cymbeline. Years of neglect and disuse had taken their toll on those few canals that penetrated the Hollows.

Most were filled with silt and refuse leaving them dry or puddled with filthy runoff after a rain.

The Grand Canal, which Canal Street followed, hardly merited the name, but at least it was full of brackish water and was still navigable after a fashion. The winter's ice had melted leaving the canal choked with floating refuse that the spring rains had yet to wash away.

Simon cruised north past row after row of old warehouses and abandoned boathouses. Most of the warehouses had been converted to tenements and flickering lights inside the boathouses marked where squatters were sheltering from the early spring cold and wet. He crossed the bridge onto Tanner Street and turned left, toward the government district.

He yawned and decided to go home first before checking in at Wycliffe House, the Peacekeeper Forces main headquarters. *A shower and a clean pair of hose are worth two hours of sleep, right?*

He parked the black sports sled in the stables behind the converted mews where he had his small flat. He'd never needed much in the way of living space or creature comforts. The flat had two rooms and a bath, the main room doing duty as sitting room, dining area and kitchen. Down a short hallway opposite the front door there was an eight by ten foot bedroom to the right and a small bathroom to the left. The bedroom furniture was sparse and simple, just a bed and a tall narrow chest of drawers. Several hooks on the wall opposite the bed provided hanging space for Simon's uniforms, sword belt, and a heavy Glenharrow wool overcoat.

Simon sat on the bed and pulled off his boots. He shed the civilian clothes he'd worn on leave and left them in a pile on the floor. He crossed to the bath and turned on the shower. Ten minutes of standing under scalding hot water left him scrubbed and revived. He still didn't feel clean. The pale faces of the dead children stared back at him whenever he closed his eyes.

Get back on the straight, Buckley. You're tired, that's all. It's just another case.

He dried off and took a clean uniform from a hook near his bed and fresh hose from a drawer. He dressed quickly in the dark blue serge breeches, blue wool hose, white shirt and blue jacket that comprised his winter uniform, the weather still too cool for the summer weight cotton. He hung the lanyard with his badge and identification medallion from his left shoulder strap and buckled on a black sword belt. Sylvie had given him a new saber, a Gallinberg Reaper, as a New Year's gift. She'd meant it to replace the Bonecleaver Mark 3 short sword he'd lost on the last case they'd worked together. She felt responsible since the sword was in her flat when Azeri terrorists had raided it and taken her prisoner. The Azeris had taken the sword, too, but it had never been recovered.

Simon looked at the slim, curved blade of the Reaper for a second before sliding it back into its scabbard. His sword skills were marginal at best and the Gallinberg was an expert's weapon, fast and deadly in the right hands. He felt slightly ridiculous carrying it, but Sylvie had convinced him that it was a symbol of his authority as a Sergeant in the Kings Peacekeepers. Besides, she'd promised to give him fencing lessons. He smiled at that prospect and buckled the scabbard to his sword belt.

The thought of Sylvie caused him to pick up his mirror and enter her locus. She responded to the summoning almost immediately. She must have been on her way to work herself because she wore the charcoal gray uniform of the Special Enforcement Division or Gray Rangers, the Elven equivalent to the Peacekeepers. Simon blinked in surprise; she had said she had two days leave remaining when he had left her.

"Simon." Her bright smile filled his mirror. "Is everything all good? You look tired."

Sylvie Graystorm, youngest daughter of *Syr* Berland Graystorm, cousin and advisor to the Steward of Tintagel, had the fine ageless features, platinum hair, and emerald green eyes of a High Elf. Just now her hair was pulled back and tied behind her curved and finely pointed ears. Her eyes searched Simon's with obvious concern.

"All good," he said. "Made it back to the capitol safely. We've caught a bad case, but it's too early to tell how bad." He told her briefly about the dead children and his and Hal's concerns about Blood magic being involved.

"More Portal spells?" Sylvie asked.

Simon shuddered at the mention of Portals. The last case he and Sylvie had worked together had involved Blood spells that opened gateways to other worlds. Worlds like their own but different. He still had the strange hand weapon from one of those other places stored in a strongbox in his locker at Wycliffe House. "I don't know. I'm hoping Kyle Evarts and Liam can tell me more once they do the forensics." He paused. "Sorry to run out on you like that."

"Don't be silly, Simon. It's the job. We both know how it is." She smiled. "Besides, I'd have been the one apologizing to you this morning. Something's come up back at Borderlands Station and I've been recalled."

"Anything serious?" he asked.

Sylvie grimaced. "Won't know until I get there." Her expression softened. "Take care, love. I enjoyed the last two days. We will be together again, I promise."

Before Simon could reply, she canceled the spell, breaking the connection. He put away his mirror and picked up his cap. When he and Sylvie were together, there seemed no room for doubt. And yet, after a night or two, he could feel her pull away. Physically, she responded to him as always, but he could feel part of her close off from him, from the shared emotion they felt at each reunion. He resolved for the hundredth time to tell her how he felt and ask her what she wanted from their uncertain relationship.

He shook his head as he closed and locked his apartment door. Who was he kidding? A Human loving an Elf was a classic prescription for heartache.

Half way to Wycliffe House a thought occurred to him. *Lily had said she'd seen one of the boys out and about alone on the street. But why was that unusual?* There were plenty of Orc urchins prowling the streets of the Hollows, looking for any opportunity to earn a few coins. Most of them had families. Indeed, their families often relied on their meager earnings to help make ends meet. *So why had Lily noticed a particular boy?*

Simon turned left off of Tanner Street a few blocks short of the stable entrance to Wycliffe House and picked up the southbound lanes of Canal Street. He reached Lily's tavern ten minutes later and pulled to the curb near the front entrance. He locked the sled, and muttered the words to activate the anti-theft Warding spell. Pushing open the door to the tavern, he stood for a moment, letting his eyes adjust to the dim lighting.

The large tavern building covered half the city block on which it sat. The common room occupied more than three quarters of the ground floor space. A long bar stood across from the street entrance with a staircase leading to the upper floors beside it on the left and wide swinging double doors leading to the kitchen on the right. The center of the huge room was broken by two pairs of heavy wooden columns that supported the floors above. Down the natural aisle between the columns were three rows of long trestle tables and benches. The walls around the room were reserved for smaller tables and a series of booths that offered more private seating. The fires in the three stone hearths along the walls had burned down to embers. The room was cool but not uncomfortably cold.

It was still early morning, just a little past seventh hour, but several clusters of people sat at the long narrow tables that filled the center of the common room. Simon saw mostly Orc laborers and tradesmen, breaking their fast and sipping strong Azeri coffee before heading out to start their workday. The low buzz of conversation died as the he entered.

He crossed the room to speak to Hack, Lily's barman and a long time employee who knew Simon well. Human, though short and broad, build more like a Dwarf, Hack's bald head shone under a row of glowglobes above the bar. His face looked pale and washed out in the artificial light. He watched Simon approach, all the while polishing the already gleaming dark wood of the bar top with a white cloth.

"Good meeting, Hack. A pint of small beer, please." Simon tossed a crown on the counter as payment and said in a lower voice, "And I'll be needing a word with your Mistress."

Hack nodded, swept up the coin and turned to the tap to draw Simon's pint. He slid it across the polished bartop before making a show of shaking out the towel in his hand, regarding it critically, and tossing it into the sink next to the taps. He went to a cupboard at the end of the bar and took out a fresh towel, then stuck his head through the kitchen door and spoke a few words before returning to his place.

Simon surveyed the common room, smiling amiably at no one in particular, and sipped his beer. The people in the room turned back to their breakfasts and the buzz of low voices resumed.

A few minutes later, a small Orc girl came out of the kitchen and tentatively approached, eyes down. She glanced at Hack who motioned with his hand toward Simon. She looked up.

"Please sir," she said. "My Mistress asks if you'd come with me to the kitchen."

Simon drained his beer, set the mug on the bar, and smiled at the girl. "Lead on," he said.

He followed her through the double swinging doors into the kitchen. The room was hot, a sharp contrast to the cool common room and the cold outside air. Two huge stoves flanked the rear door where Simon had spoken to Frank Killian a few hours before. A cauldron of porridge steamed on one, while two large black coffee pots bubbled away on the other, their handles wrapped in colorful cotton dishtowels. Lily sat alone at a planked worktable in the center of the room. Half cut loaves of bread, rashers of raw bacon and a dozen eggs nestled in a box of wood shavings lay around the small cleared space in front of her. She'd obviously sent the cooks and serving maids out before sending the girl to fetch him.

"Thank you, Merti," Lily said to the girl. "Now go help Hack with washing the tables."

The girl nodded and fled without another word, intimidated either by her Mistress or by Simon's presence.

"You wished to speak to me, Sergeant?" Lily asked stiffly after the girl was gone. She didn't ask Simon to sit and he didn't see another chair anyway. Her formality took him by surprise. There had always been a barrier between them, even when Simon had been walking a beat in the neighborhood as a common Patrol Keeper, but he had thought they had reached an understanding. It wasn't like Lily was a friend, more of an ally in a common cause. This formality made him uneasy.

"I wanted to speak to you about the dead children," he said. She stiffened, and he went on. "You know more than you've said, at least about the girl who occasionally worked for you, and the boy you mentioned. I hoped a quiet conversation between the two of us would make it easier for you to tell me more."

Lily stared at him for a second, then glanced at the back door before looking down at the tabletop. "The girls name was Seri. The boy was her brother. Jochim, I think his name was. Some time back, their parents disappeared from

28

a houseboat about three blocks from here. No one knows where they went. Like I said, I used to let her sweep up now and then in return for some left over food. I hadn't seen either of them for a couple of months before they ended up in my back lot with their throats cut."

"Parents' names?" Simon asked.

Lily shrugged. "Family name was Marshstrider, but they were Azeri, I think. Maybe second generation. Never knew their given names."

"Why didn't you give that information to Killian?" he asked. "Or to me, last night?"

Lily cocked her head and looked at him as if considering how to answer. Before she could say anything, there was a loud triple knock at the back door.

Lily's expression changed to one of alarm, and she made a shooing gesture at Simon. When he stood his ground, she sighed and went to the door. She turned the handle and the door was pushed open from the other side.

A very young woman in a richly embroidered green cloak swept into the room followed closely by a tall man in the uniform of the Royal Security Service. Simon immediately recognized the scarred, lopsided face of Lieutenant Stenson Harold. Harold saw Simon and frowned. He reached out toward the young woman but she was already beyond his grasp, clutching Lily in a tight embrace. The hood of the cloak fell back and revealed a cascade of golden blond hair.

Simon gasped in recognition and looked at Harold, who stepped closer to Simon, never taking his eyes off of the young woman.

"What the hells are you doing here, Buckley?" Harold asked in a hoarse whisper.

"Questioning a material witness," said Simon. "What the hells is she doing here?"

"Whatever she likes," said Harold ruefully. "She is the Princess, after all."

Princess Rebeka Fangbern, only daughter of King

Thorston Fangbern, stepped back from her embrace of Lily Ponsaka but stood close to the short Orc woman, clasping both of her hands.

"Is it true, Lily?" she asked, her voice husky. "About Seri and Jochim?"

"Aye, your Highness," said Lily. "I myself saw them and knew them for certain."

"But how?" asked Rebeka. "They were supposed to be at the Cloister. They were safe there. Why would they leave?"

"I don't know, M'lady." Lily squeezed the younger woman's hands. "I tried to summon Mr. Silverlake by mirror, but he hasn't answered me. The matron says they left of their own accord some days ago, but couldn't say why or if they went with anyone else."

"You've been holding out on me, Lily," said Simon, now truly angry. "I thought we'd gotten past this type of dreck. You pester Hal and Killian to get us assigned to this case and then you leave me up a blind tunnel?"

Before Lily could answer, Princess Rebeka turned and regarded him coolly. She had the golden blond hair and piercing green eyes of her father, but where the King and Crown Prince both inclined to plumpness, the Princess had a lean angular build. Her high cheekbones and large eyes spoke to her mother's Half-Elven side while her full lips and slightly enlarged front teeth were all her father's. The combination made her striking, if not classically beautiful.

"And you are?" she asked.

"I'm Simon Buckley, Sergeant Simon Buckley of the Magic Enforcement squad." Simon bowed somewhat belatedly. He gave Lily a sharp look. "Mistress Ponsaka is a material witness in a case of illegal conjuring. She's the reason I'm on this case and I don't appreciate being kept in the dark about critical information."

"I couldn't talk to you until Her Highness knew what had happened." Lily, wrung her hands on her apron. "She was involved with those two kids and I needed to warn her before telling you about them."

Rebeka looked from Simon to Lily, her face pale. "Lily, what's he talking about? I heard that Seri and Jochim were dead. What does that have to do with illegal magic?"

"Seri and Jochim and two other Orc children were killed as part of a Blood magic ritual," said Simon. "What can you tell me about them, since Lily here doesn't want to reveal anything."

Rebeka stared at him, her lips parted in a small "O" of surprise and shock. Then her eyelids fluttered and her knees buckled. Lily and Harold stepped to her side and supported her arms as she recovered somewhat and tried to straighten.

"Tactful as ever, Buckley," muttered Harold as he steered the Princess to the chair where Lily had been sitting earlier.

Simon felt a hot flush in his face and then a slight pinging sensation at the base of his spine. The dishcloths wrapped around the handles of the large coffee pots behind Lily burst into flames.

CHAPTER FOUR

"Durlash's Beard!" cried Lily, rushing to douse the flames with a pitcher of water.

Harold got Rebeka into the chair. She hadn't fainted, Simon noted, but seemed to be unaware of those around her. The episode lasted only a few seconds. By the time Harold got her seated in the chair her eyes were clear, although the stricken look on her face had not changed.

Lily approached again, muttering under her breath. She held a mug of hot coffee that she offered to Rebeka. "The cloth must have come loose, touched the stovetop, caught fire," she said. "No harm done. Drink M'lady. It'll do you good."

Rebeka accepted the mug and sipped the hot liquid, clutching the cup in both hands. "Blood magic?" She kept her eyes on Simon. "What sort of Blood magic?"

Simon glanced at Harold before answering. "We don't know. But Mistress Ponsaka first noted the signs and made sure my team was summoned. What can you tell me about Seri and Jochim? And who else knew what you and Lily were doing here?"

"They were . . ." Rebeka started, then stopped. "What are you implying? Lily and I were trying to help these children."

"Help them how?"

"By feeding them, clothing them, finding safe places for them to stay." Rebeka's eyes flashed and her face colored. "No one cares about abandoned Orc children. Throwaway's, they're called. As if they were trash to be discarded. My father's Social Welfare Ministry barely acknowledges they exist, and then willfully underreports their numbers. At least Lily and her people understand the problem."

Simon held up a hand. "I get it. You obviously feel strongly about them. But I need to know about Seri and Jochim specifically. You mentioned a place called the Cloister. What is that? Someplace that takes in these children?"

Rebeka set the coffee on the worktable and folded her arms, glaring at Simon. It was Lily who spoke up. "It's a school in the Northwest Territory, near the border." She ignored the glare that Rebeka was now directing her way.

"A school for Orc children?" Simon asked.

"What?" sneered Rebeka. "Because they're Orcs, they shouldn't get an education?"

Simon turned to her, controlling his sudden anger. He spoke slowly and carefully. "Your Highness, I grew up in Westport, on the docks. I went to a Kings School along with all the other children in the district, Orc, Human or Dwarf. We all got the same education." He paused and looked from Rebeka to Lily. "None of us could afford to go to one of the private academies. And for certain none of us dreamed about attending a boarding school way off in the Northwest."

"It isn't that kind of school," Lily said.

"What kind is it?" asked Simon, the edge still in his

voice.

Lily blushed. "Not that kind either. They take in Orc kids with no family—orphans, lost kids, throwaways. They teach them basic letters and figures, give them a trade, a start."

"Who does the funding? It's not a King's School, not one that I've ever heard of."

Lily looked away "They make do. The kids do their part, too." To Simon's skeptical look, she added. "It's better than the streets,"

'They get decent food, a warm bed, safety, and honest work." Rebeka jutted out her chin. "They get hope. What have you and your Peacekeepers done to help? Their parents turned them out, ten or twelve year old children, to fend for themselves. Somebody has to do something."

Simon flashed on a memory of hiding in the crawl space under the floor of his father's ship chandlery, the smell of burning sailcloth in his nose, as the Azeri gang smashed the windows and looted the storeroom. He'd only spent a few nights on the street as an orphan, hiding from the Orcs who had killed his father, before Hal had found him and taken him in. He could imagine the despair of children left alone for days and weeks on end. His anger at the Princess abated.

"We do what we can, Your Highness," he said, and something about his tone or the expression on his face made her stop and look at him.

"Yes, we do," she answered quietly.

"So," Simon turned to face Lily "What about Seri and Jochim? You said they were at the Cloister. How did they end up here?"

Rebeka glanced at Lily as well. "I honestly don't know." The Orc woman hung her head. "We thought they were safe. Off the street. But when I saw them here, like that." She waved a hand vaguely at the back door. "I knew something was wrong."

"You told Rebeka that you spoke to a matron," said Simon. "At the school?"

"Aye," Lily said. "She said they had left there some days ago, of their own accord. She didn't know more than that. She hadn't been on duty when they left. I asked to talk to Mr. Silverlake but he wasn't at the school. Some sort of fundraising trip. I've left messages everywhere I can think of for him to summon my mirror as soon as possible."

"Who is Silverlake?" Simon asked.

"Hiramis Silverlake," answered Rebeka. "He's the school's Headmaster."

"Orc?"

Rebeka shook her head. "He's an Elf, of the Free People, not the Havens."

"Why does an Elf, even one of the Free People, run a school for Orc children?" asked Simon, as much to himself as to the Princess.

"Maybe because he has a social conscience." Rebeka's voice grew harsh with renewed indignation.

Simon held up his hands. "No offense intended, Your Highness. You must admit, it's not common for any Elf, even one of the Free People, to be concerned about Orcs. Hiramis Silverlake is unusual if only for that reason. And, in an investigation like this, the unusual is sometimes important."

"His reasons are his own, Sergeant," the Princess said, not mollified. "I have never asked."

"He's done a lot of good, Simon," added Lily quickly. "We've been working with him near on three years now. Why, one of my cooks came to me from the Cloister, as did Harska Froncek's apprentice. He's the tailor, two buildings north of me. Says the lad is game and reliable and already knows more stitchery than any of the other workers in his shop. Whatever happened to those kids, I can't see Hiramis Silverlake being involved in it."

"But the last you knew of Seri and Jochim, they were at

the Cloister?" Simon asked.

Lily nodded.

"Then we'll be needing a word with your Mr. Silverlake." Simon turned to Rebeka, who was still glaring at him, her arms tightly folded across her chest.

"What more can you tell me about Seri and Jochim?" he asked her. "How did they get to the Cloister? How was it all arranged? And how does Silverlake determine which children he admits to the school?"

"Am I under caution, Sergeant?" she asked. "Am I a suspect or a material witness in your case?"

"Not as of now, Your Highness," he answered.

"Then I choose to exercise my right not to answer your questions." She turned to Lily. "I'll be in touch, Lily. And I will take care of any costs for the death rituals." She squeezed Lily's shoulder briefly then brushed past Simon toward the door. "We're leaving, Stenson."

Harold smiled at Simon. "Sorry, Buckley. She can be a handful, but she knows her rights. File a request with Palace Security and I'll try to get you an official interview once she's had time to think about this. And for once, I agree with you. She likely has useful information, whether she realizes it or not." He paused to button his coat and adjust his cap. "Good parting, Sergeant Buckley."

"Good parting, Lieutenant Harold," said Simon. "I'll be in touch."

Harold threw him a mock salute and followed the Princess out the door.

Simon looked at Lily. "What about it, Lily? Can you tell me any more about Silverlake and this school?"

"Not much," she answered. "Rebeka first brought him to us. I would pick out some likely kids, ones who hadn't gotten into major trouble or been too long on the street. I'd tell Rebeka and she'd talk to the children herself. Then one of Silverlake's people, always an Orc, would come down and check the kids out. If it seemed a good fit, they'd talk to the kids, tell them about the school. Make sure they knew what would be expected of them." She paused and wiped at a smudge on the work table. "The school isn't a picnic in the park, you know. But it beats the street. Anyway, if the children were willing, they'd get a coach ticket and directions to the Cloister in a couple of weeks."

"How would they get them? By mail?"

Lily shook her head. "Courier service would deliver them here and I'd pass them on. The kids knew to check with me every day."

"You've never been to the school yourself?" Simon asked.

"Never had time. Got this place to run, don't I?" Lily's eyes narrowed at the skeptical look on Simon's face. "Just because I never went there doesn't mean I don't know about it. Like I said, Ciara, my cook, learned her craft there. She can tell you about it."

Simon rubbed his eyes, the fatigue suddenly catching up with him. "Some other time. What about Seri and Jochim in particular? Why would they leave the school? Could they have been unhappy there?"

Lily raised her hands, a look of anguish on her face. "I don't know Simon, hand to the gods, I don't know. They weren't really street kids. Their parents may have gone missing, but them kids had been cared for. Seri was older, but Jochim thought he was the man of the family and had to watch out for her. It used to make her so angry sometimes." She stopped and put a hand on her forehead. "They weren't bad kids, Simon. Just poor. They didn't deserve what happened to them."

"I know, Lily. No one does."

"Then you'll look into it?" she asked. "Now that it's a case of Blood magic and not just a bunch of dead throwaway kids?"

"I'd have looked into it anyway, Lily." Simon shifted and touched her gently on the shoulder. "Even before I moved to Magic Enforcement. Killian would have, too, you know."

"I suppose you're right," Lily sighed. "He's the best we've had down here in a long while. The best since you stopped walking a beat, truth be told."

"Killian's basically honest. He's an ambitious climber, but not a bad Keeper." Simon smiled. "Just thick as swamp mud sometimes."

Lily smiled back on hearing her own words. "How did he end up here, if I can ask? Didn't he used to be a Sergeant, like you?"

"He got mixed up in something political. Something way above his rank. He's lucky he kept his badge, which is why he's going to be very careful to follow all the rules for a while. He'd love to solve a case like this and get back his rank." Simon held up a finger for emphasis. "He'll do the right thing, but you shouldn't trust him."

"Like I'd trust any Bluebelly?" Lily's smile broadened.

"Fair enough." Simon laughed. "We'll want to talk with your cook eventually. I'll have Kermal Brackenville come by tomorrow."

"I'll make sure Ciara is here," Lily said.

"All good then." Simon turned to go but then stopped. "You said Seri and Jochim had been at the school for a while?"

"A couple of months," answered Lily.

"Do you know anything more about the parents? Clan, for instance?"

"Ox Clan, I think. Why?"

"My armorer thinks the girl had worn a ceremonial headdress recently. Seri looks like she'd have been the right age for a Naming Ceremony."

Lily nodded. "She was. She spoke about it once, about how she wouldn't have a real name because her parents weren't there to speak it for her."

"Would the Cloister have held a ceremony for her?"

"I don't know. The school tried to keep things Orcish whenever possible. Maybe Ciara could tell you if they did such things."

Simon held out a hand. "Thank you, Lily. We'll do our best to find out what happened to your kids."

Lily shook his hand, her face grim. "Good parting, Simon," she said. "I'll be waiting to hear from you."

CHAPTER FIVE

Simon left Lily in the kitchen and crossed the now busy common room. More people sat at the tables and several serving girls roamed among them with pots of coffee and cauldrons of porridge. Hack had made up the fires and the room was pleasantly warm. In earlier times, when he had patrolled the streets in the neighborhood, he'd have lingered here with a mug of coffee, letting himself be seen, friendly and relaxed. Now he was an outsider, ignored by most, watched with suspicion by some and open hostility by a few. He felt a pang of loneliness.

Those early days had been hard, but he'd felt part of a community then. He was closer than ever to Hal and the rest of his team now, but the loss of Ham and the changes in the squad room after Gulbrandsen's downfall had driven a wedge between his team and the rank and file Keepers on the Force. Some blamed the team for breaking the unspoken rule that Keepers always covered for each other; even those who understood that some things couldn't be covered up were shaken by the depth of Gulbrandsen's betrayal.

Can't be helped, Simon thought.

As he approached the door, two large Orcs stood up from a nearby table and blocked his path. He stopped just out of their reach, settling his weight on the balls of his feet and shifting into a fencer's stance. He thought he could draw his needler and take the one on the right, but the second one would be on him before he would get a second shot. *Two against one in a crowded barroom isn't the way I want to start this day. But I don't think these hardboys much care about that.* Still, he made no move toward his needler or the Reaper at his left hip. He waited, nerves taut, for them to declare their intentions.

The Orcs, Canal Street Scalpers by the look of their tattoos and the shapeless red knit caps they wore, stood with their hands held out from their sides, palms outward.

"Rein in, Keeper," said the Orc on Simon's right. "No harm here. Mr. Kronska just wants a word." He gestured farther to the right where a third Orc sat at a table, half concealed in the shadows.

Simon looked closer and recognized Farsk Kronska seated with his back to the wall. A plate of eggs and smoked fish sat before him, along with two steaming mugs of coffee. Simon inclined his head and Kronska touched the side of his large hooked nose in response.

The Orc who had spoken stepped back a pace and made a gesture toward the table. Simon eased off the balls of his feet, but still on alert, walked over, and pulled out the chair opposite Kronska.

"*Mr. Kronska,* is it now, Nose?" Simon asked with a hint of sarcasm as he sat down. Farsk "Nose" Kronska had been a midlevel soldier for the Scalpers back when Simon had been on foot Patrol. They'd developed a kind of mutual respect in those days; not friendship, but recognition of each other's role in the big picture.

41

"Aye, it is," said Kronska. "I've come up in the world a piece, as have you *Sergeant* Buckley. Have some coffee. Lily's is the best you'll get, south of Tanner."

Simon took the nearest mug and sipped. Food offered and accepted, he was free to talk business. "What do you want, Nose?" he asked.

"We need to clear the waters about them dead kids." Kronska stirred his coffee. "Your boy Killian is putting it out that the Loblollies done for them as some kind of message to me."

Simon sipped the hot brew, savoring the heat and hoping the coffee would replace the sleep he'd missed. "He's wrong?"

"Damn certain, he is."

"SP Killian thinks the Loblollies wanted to warn you off of their jolt territory." Simon looked into his mug as if reading something in the dark liquid. "As I hear it, you've got dealers selling as far west as the Old Wall. That's Knacker Street territory."

"Why would the 'Lollies kill some throwaways and leave them at Lily's to send me a message? Better they cut up a couple of my boys and drop them on the Knacker Street bridge, if that's what they wanted to say." Kronska shook his head. "Them kids got nothing to do with me and my business with the Loblollies."

Simon swirled his coffee and watched the pattern in the grounds as he considered the Orc's words.. He looked up at Kronska. "Why tell me this?"

"Because you're on the straight and you ain't looking to make a name like Killian is. He's been down on me and mine since he got busted to this beat." Kronska forked eggs and fish into his mouth. He swallowed, gulped some coffee, and pointed at Simon with his fork. "You were always square with me when you had the beat here. Not soft, not by a long shot, but you never busted heads unless they needed busting. Killian's different. Likes nothing better than kicking a few Orcs around to start his day. Let him run with that story and the 'Lollies will start thinking I'm the one putting it out. Maybe think I'm setting up for a push into the west end."

"And you're not?" Simon leaned forward. "You're selling jolt in their back garden. I hear you've poached a few of their best markets in the last couple of months."

Kronska ate more eggs and waved dismissively. "Small time action. Goes on all the time. They sell their stuff over by the stockyards. Not officially Scalper property, but ours by reputation. So I take a couple of corners away from them, just to even up. They set a couple of fires in my warehouse, I tip off the Bluebellies about their shipments. And we're even again. That's different from a full scale war, and that's what Biran Stillwater will be looking to start if he thinks I'm about to hit him first."

"So what do you want from me?"

"Put it out that it was Blood magic what killed them kids, not the 'Lollies," said Kronska.

"You sure it wasn't Stillwater's people? Does he have any Blood mages in the gang?" Simon kept his tone even.

"What? No! No more'n I do."

"And you don't?"

"No, by Durlash." Kronska shuddered. "Won't abide it. Not in my crew, I won't."

"What if Stillwater isn't buying?"

Kronska rubbed his chin. "I might could arrange a face to face, here at Lily's. It's neutral ground. If you're here to set him straight, it won't be just street noise, and he can see I ain't just covering my ass."

"I'll come," Simon agreed. "I want to talk to Stillwater myself. The other two kids may be from somewhere in his territory."

"All I ask." Kronska gulped some more coffee. "Water's clear, yes?

"Clear." Simon stood to leave, but stopped. "What fires?"

"Eh?" Kronska looked up at him, puzzled.

"You said the 'Lollies started a couple of fires. When? Where?"

The Orc waved a hand "Few days back, a couple of fires started in the old warehouses down by the Canal. Not much damage, just lost a bit of product."

"And Stillwater's people started them?" asked Simon.

"Fire Brigade said arson, so figure it has to be 'Lollies what set 'em."

Simon nodded. "Killian know about it?"

Kronska shook his head. "Couldn't say. Not that he'd care much about a hundredweight of jolt off the street. Nobody hurt except me and my business."

"You want me to look into it, Nose?"

"Nah, I can watch out for my own. Besides, won't do to have Bluebellies meddling in Orc business." He finished the last of the eggs and raised the coffee mug in a mock toast. "Take care, Sergeant Buckley. I'll be in touch."

Simon tapped a finger to the side of his nose. Without another word, he turned and brushed past the two Scalpers by the door.

He took a deep breath of cold air once he was on the sidewalk and walked slowly toward his Oxley. He'd have to have a talk with Frank Killian. Despite Simon's rank, he wasn't in Killian's chain of command. He couldn't order him to do anything outside of the narrow confines of this particular investigation. It was clear that the rivalry between the Scalpers and the Loblollies had heated up since Simon's time on the street. Kronska wouldn't have reached out unless he was truly concerned that the dead children could be the spark that started a war between the gangs. Simon didn't know if Killian was deliberately provoking the Loblollies, or if, as Lily said, he was simply as thick as swamp mud. Either way, he'd need to be part of any negotiation between Kronska and Stillwater.

I don't like it, but it is Killian's beat. He'll have to be in on it.

By the time he turned west onto Tanner Street and approached Wycliffe House, it was after eighth hour. Even in the bright sunshine of a spring morning, Wycliffe House looked forbidding. During its five hundred year history, it had been a fortress, a royal palace, an armory, and, most notably, a prison. During the Magisterium, Wycliffe House had been synonymous with despair, torture, and dark magic. The Restoration and establishment of the Commonwealth Accords under King Otto, one hundred and seventy years ago, had emptied Wycliffe's dungeons and torn down the thick walls and the bailey that had surrounded it. On the north side, the old moat and forecourt had been filled and turned into a greenbelt. Holes had been cut in the north face of the old fortress and huge glass windows installed to symbolize the enlightenment of the new order. On the south side, however, what Simon thought of as the working entrance to Wycliffe House, the gray granite walls rose sheer from the street level, broken only by narrow arrow slit windows and barred postern doors. Here, the House retained its dark face and promised no mercy to the King's enemies.

Simon turned into the entrance to the underground stables and drove down the ramp to the parking area for personal sleds. There were few spaces left this late in the morning—Peacekeeper shifts started at seventh hour—and Simon had to carefully wedge his Tornado between a big Hilten six-seat sedan and an old Finn utility sled. He recognized the Finn as Jack Ironhand's and wondered if Hal was here as well.

He climbed the ancient stone stairway, ignoring the stiffness from the lack of sleep, past the ground floor holding cells and booking rooms to the squad room on the second floor. The day watch was already at work, busy with FarSpeaker calls, scribbling notes, and checking updates on their mirrors. The room smelled of burned coffee, stale smoke and a century of human traffic. On the far wall, a large magic mirror was tuned to a 24-hour news network.

Hal and Jack weren't at their desks. Simon crossed the room, waving good meeting to day watch agents he knew and tossing a salute at Lieutenant Servi Lillihammer, the day watch commander. She returned it absently and went back to her FS call. In the far corner of the large room, a partition of frosted glass and wood walled off an eight by six foot enclosure that was his office. He heard Hal and Jack before he reached the entrance to the small space.

"Reba's worried, Jack," Hal said. "She knows you couldn't have done anything to save Ham. She's afraid you're looking for something from her that she can't give."

"I don't want anything but what's best for her and the kids." Jack's voice was hoarse with grief. "It's what I promised Ham. It's up to me to see they don't want for anything."

"West Wray ain't the Darrowdowns, lad," sighed Hal. "Humans don't see things the same. Reba's grieving her husband, sure, but she has a need to move on, to find her own way."

"Ham's only three months dead," said Jack.

"For Humans that can be a long time," Hal said softly. "Let her be, Jack. She'll ask for help if she needs it."

"Three months," repeated Jack. "Feels like I'm betraying my friend. Reba's got a job, you know. And the kids still call me Uncle Jack, but you can tell it's not the same as when I'd be there with their Da. Even the team is moving on, leaving Ham behind."

"Team is different," said Hal. "We've had replacements before. Can't leave us understrength for long. Besides, for an Orc, Brackenville's not a bad Keeper."

"It ain't that he's an Orc." Jack's hoarse voice, barely rose above a whisper. "It's that he ain't Ham."

Simon coughed before approaching the open door to the office. He stepped in to find Hal leaning against the outer wall and Jack sitting on the battered couch that faced Simon's cluttered desk. No one spoke, and Simon wouldn't shame Jack by letting on that he'd heard the grief in his voice. Not that they didn't all feel it, each grieving in his own way. He slid into the old wooden chair behind the desk and greeted Jack.

"Anything useful from the neighborhood canvass?" he asked.

"Maybe," said Jack, his voice now strong and even. "A tailor, Orc by the name of Froncek, says he saw a green commercial sledge pull around the corner at Canal and Knacker and head north in a big hurry. He remembers because it almost hit him as he was crossing Canal leaving Lily's place. He didn't see the registry number and said the windscreen was blacked out; didn't see the driver either. He thinks it was a Hilten panel sledge." Jack consulted a small notebook from his pocket. "He also thinks there was a commercial sigil on the side of it, some sort of interlocked Elfscript."

"What did it say?"

"Froncek didn't know, said he doesn't read Elfscript." Jack shrugged. "Frankly, Sarge, the guy was still half drunk when I talked to him. He must have been pretty toasted when he left Lily's. I'm not sure we should put much stock in his story."

"Perhaps not," Simon said. "But it's the only lead we've got right now, unless Kermal learns something more about the girl." He saw the look of pain that crossed Jacks face. "I know he's not Ham, Jack. But he's smart and knows his weapons. The team needs an armorer."

Jack shifted in his seat but said nothing.

"Go talk to Lieutenant Lillehammer. She has a contact in the Merchant's Guild who knows just about every business sigil and guild badge in the Commonwealth. Get some images of Elf sigils to show to this tailor. See if he recognizes one of them."

Jack nodded. Simon turned and looked at Hal.

"I went back and talked to Lily again, like you suggested. She knew a lot more than she had said." Simon quickly told Hal and Jack about his conversation with Lily and Princess Rebeka's involvement with the children.

Hal let out a low whistle. "The Crown Princess, don't you say. That puts a kink in the tunnel, no doubt about it."

"Lieutenant Harold said he would try to talk some sense into her and suggested we request an interview through Palace security. It's that or we go to the King's Prosecutor for a subpoena."

Hal laughed. "You'd best be looking for another line of work if you take this to the KP. No, lad. We do as Harold suggested. It'll take a few days, but it's more politic."

"You're right," Simon agreed. "Meanwhile, we have names, a clan, and maybe a family name. I'll get the records guys on it."

"Don't expect too much," said Kermal Brackenville from the door. Simon hadn't heard him approach and wondered what he'd overheard.

Jack looked up and grunted. Hal looked at Simon and sighed.

"Good meeting, Brackenville," Hal said neutrally. "What do you mean?"

Kermal looked from Simon to Hal and paused a half second before answering.

Maybe he did hear us, Simon thought.

"They likely weren't citizens, or even registered immigrants. Most of the Azeris down in the Hollows are refugees without papers. They change their names, work for cash and generally try to avoid any official notice. It's part of the reason the throwaway kids never get any attention."

"Did you learn anything in the East End?" Simon asked.

"A few things," Kermal answered, still watching Hal. "More than a dozen kids have gone missing over the past few months. Not throwaways or orphans, but kids with families."

"Did they get reported?" asked Hal.

"Two or three." Kermal shifted his stance to take in the rest of the office "The rest, no. Folks out that way have no love for the Keepers. I'm sure some are runaways, leaving home for the thrill of it, or looking for something better." He paused, looking from Simon to Hal again. "But there's a feeling on the street that Orcs, and Ox clan in particular, are being targeted and that the authorities don't care. No one has any clear idea who is responsible."

"The missing children were all Ox clan?" Simon found he wasn't surprised at the link to the dead girl and boy outside Lily's. This confirmed his gut feeling that there was a bigger picture behind the four Orc children

"The most of them," said Kermal. "It's why folks out there were so willing to talk to me, don't you see. I told them one of the dead girls was Ox. "

"Did you learn anything about the girl?"

Kermal shook his head. "No, not specifically. No one I talked to seemed to know the family. And no one knew of any recent Naming Ceremony in the area. I did get the name of a craftsman up on the north side of All God's Square who makes most of the headdresses the Clan uses. We can check his order book for the past month or so"

"Good." Hal gave him a genuine smile. "Slim lead, but better than a dark tunnel with no lamp."

Simon suppressed a grin. "Good work, Kermal. Check it out after we finish here."

"Yes, s . . . Sarge, "Kermal said.

"Anything else?" Simon asked. Kermal and Jack both shook their heads. "Right then, get on with it. I'll find Liam and see what he learned from the forensics mages. We'll meet back here at sixteenth hour and compare notes."

Jack heaved himself up off of the couch and he and Kermal headed out into the squad room.

"Hal, could you stay a minute?" asked Simon.

Hal perched on the arm of the couch, across from Simon's desk. "Something troubling you, lad?"

"Not trouble, exactly," said Simon. "On my way out of Lily's, I had an interesting talk with Nose Kronska."

"I hear he's taking on airs, calling himself *Mr. Kronska* now." Hal smirked.

"He is," said Simon, "But that's not what was interesting. He's worried about a war with the Loblollies. He blames Frank Killian for stirring up trouble down in the Hollows. He wants me to vet a meeting between him and Biran Stillwater and make sure Stillwater knows he doesn't think the 'Lollies killed those kids as a warning to the Scalpers."

"Frank won't be happy about that." Hal frowned. "He's already got a temper when it comes to outside interference with his beat, and he's got no love for you. Do this without him and he'll go straight to Axhart with it."

Captain Gelbard Axhart was the commanding Peacekeeper for the capitol city of Cymbeline. He was also doing double duty as head of the Magic Enforcement squad after the removal of Lieutenant Gulbrandsen a couple of months earlier. Axhart's only charge to Simon as a Sergeant on the squad had been to avoid any more conflict or controversy until Gulbrandsen's replacement was named. A feud with the Civil Enforcement squad would not make Axhart happy.

"I know," agreed Simon. "That's why I want you with me when I talk to Killian about it."

"Me? Are you daft, lad? Frank Killian would cut off his left foot before he'd take my advice."

"Not so, Hal," said Simon. "You've been a Keeper since before Killian went from diapers to hose and breeches. He may not like you, but he'll listen to you."

"Maybe," grumbled Hal. "You're certain Nose isn't just tossing sand?"

"No, but he's worried about Biran Stillwater. He may have his own agenda, but I get the feeling that Killian has been playing the gangs off against one another. To what end, I don't know." Simon sighed. "It's not really in our garden, but Nose and I had an understanding once. If he's reaching out now, something serious is going on."

CHAPTER SIX

Senior Patrol Agent Francis Killian sat behind a battered government-issue desk in the southeast corner of the squad room. As a Senior Agent he had the entire corner, and the narrow window, to himself. The rest of his team shared desks nearby, but were all out on patrol, staying in touch with Killian via the Peacekeeper FarSpeaker network, or by mirror for more classified discussions.

As Simon and Hal approached, Killian looked up from his mirror. He spoke a few words to whoever was on the other side of the connection and canceled the spell. He sat back in his chair and regarded Simon with narrowed eyes.

Simon met his gaze. "Have you got a few minutes, Frank?" he asked, careful to keep his tone neutral. "Something's come up that I need to talk with you about."

"About those dead Orc kids?" Killian looked from Simon to Hal.

"No, not directly. We did get identification on two of

them, brother and sister, Seri and Jochim Marshstrider. Did you ever hear the name yourself or from one of your men?"

Killian shuffled some papers on his desk. "Not that I recall. Common enough name, though. It's possible. If not them, then what?"

"I spent a little more time talking to Lily Ponsaka, which is how I found out the name of those two children. On my way out of Lily's, two of Nose Kronska's boys stopped me. I had a short talk with Nose. It seems you aren't the only one who thinks those dead children were put there by the Loblollies as a warning. Nose doesn't believe that himself, but the rumors are making the rounds."

Killian made a sour face but said nothing. Simon continued. "It's your beat, Frank. What you say down there, what you do, carries weight. Nose is worried that the Loblollies will think he's looking to start a war over the jolt trade. That he'll use these dead kids as a reason to move against Biran Stillwater."

Killian stopped pushing papers around and glared at Simon. "Knacker Street's not my beat. What Stillwater believes is none of my concern. And if he did kill those kids and put them out there for the Scalpers to see, he'll not be surprised if Kronska hits back."

"That could start a gang war between the Scalpers and the Loblollies. Is that really what you want, Frank?"

"Why should we care if a bunch of Orc hardboys knock each other off?" asked Killian. "Less trouble for my lads in the long run. And less jolt on the streets."

Hal spoke up. "In principal, I agree. But a lot of decent folk would get hurt and it would throw the drug market into a jumble. The real danger is the Azeris moving in. If the Azeri Liberation Brigades get hold of the jolt trade, they'll have money for all sorts of deviltry."

"Since when did Hal Stonebender give two shits about Orcs down in the Hollows?" sneered Killian.

Hal reddened, but held his tongue at a sign from Simon.

"Nose wants a meeting with Biran Stillwater, a face to face talk to clear the waters about the killings," said Simon. "Maybe work out a truce."

"What's that got to do with me?"

"It's your beat, Frank," Simon repeated. "Nose wants me to vet the meeting, to be there so Stillwater knows everything's on the straight. I want you there, too."

Killian gave a harsh laugh. "What, as your assistant? Like a probationer? No thanks. I'll spare myself the humiliation."

"You'll go as the ranking Civil Patrol agent on that beat," said Hal. "You'll run the meeting and Simon will be the observer."

Killian looked sharply at Hal. "Says who?".

"Says me," replied Hal. "Kronska needs to make peace, at least for a while, and you need to step up with something besides head-busting to show that the peace will be kept. Biran Stillwater and his 'Lollies hold the high ground down there. He's been in charge longer than Nose and he's got more muscle. But he doesn't want a war that would cripple his gang and leave the jolt trade open to takeover by the Azeris. Nose is new to the job and needs to firm up his hold on the Scalpers. He can't afford to look weak, but can't afford to provoke Stillwater into fighting."

"I'm the one endorsing the meeting." Simon's voice was calm but cold. "You know where I stand on the Orcs. Now, you can do as Hal says or not. Your choice. But the meeting will happen, and if you aren't there, don't expect any respect from the Scalpers, and more important, from Lily and her people."

Killian glared at him for a second, then looked away. "Right, then. I'll be there. I think you're being played for a fool, but I'll be there. When?"

"Nose will call. It'll be you, me, and any two of your lads you choose."

Killian nodded. "Anything else, Sergeant? Because if not, I've got real Keeper work to do."

Hal bristled. but Simon simply replied.

"As you say, Frank. I'm keeping you in the circle, like you asked. I'll let you know when Nose calls," Simon simply replied.

"That went well," muttered Hal as they walked away.

"Better than I expected," said Simon.

"Mighty low expectation, then. What next?"

"I want to talk to Kyle Evarts and Liam and see what they've been able to learn about those children. Maybe if we know what sort of spell they were used for, we can get a lead on who cast it."

"Right," said Hal. "Meantime, I'll see what I can find out on this school Lily told you about, and run Hiramis Silverlake through the criminal registries. If he runs a legitimate school, his ear pattern will be on record."

Simon found Liam in the morgue with Kyle Evarts. The two of them were bent over a postmortem table. A faint golden glow surrounding the small body of one of the dead children faded rapidly away as Simon pushed through the swinging door of the cold room.

"Just like the others," Liam said.

"Nothing," said Evarts. "No aura, no residual, no nothing. Frustrating."

"What's frustrating?" asked Simon.

Liam looked up from the marble topped table. "Oh, good meeting, Sarge. Kyle and I were trying a series of aural analysis spells on the victims to see if we could pinpoint a time of death."

Kyle Evarts glanced at Simon before returning his attention to the table. He was even taller than Liam with the slim build and natural grace of the Half-Elven. His hair was a shade lighter than Liam's red blond and his features were decidedly more Elven, but seeing them together, it struck Simon they were enough alike to be related, maybe older uncle and nephew.

"Decomp and body temp are consistent with about twenty hours before they were discovered," Evarts said. "With that time frame, I hoped to do aural analysis to pin down the exact moment of death."

"And?"

"There's no residual life aura in any of the children." Evarts gave him a puzzled look. "That shouldn't be possible. The life aura fades at a predictable rate after death. There are logarithms based on age, race, and cause of death. They can be fairly complex, but the spell mechanics are well researched and standardized. We should see a faint but unique aura for each of these children. But there's nothing."

"What about the glow I saw when I came in?" asked Simon.

"That was a residual of the Blood spell cast when they died," said Evarts. "It's definitely a Fire spell of some sort, which is a bit odd since most Blood curses are Earth spells."

Liam rubbed his chin. "I vaguely recall one of my mentors mentioning a family of Fire based Blood spells, but nothing specific. With no residual life aura, I'd be tempted to say they were dead for a while before their blood was drained, but the bruising under the skin near the wounds indicates they were alive when they were cut. It's like whatever Blood spell they were killed for completely drained all life from them, even the aura."

"Is that even possible?" Simon was no mage, but he'd studied enough magical theory to know that what Liam was describing would be highly unlikely.

Liam cocked his head. "I wouldn't have said so yesterday. Now, I don't know."

Simon looked down on the frail body on the marble slab. Seri, the girl who had worked for Lily. "She was alive when they did this?" His voice was barely above a whisper.

"Yes," said Liam. "Likely she was sedated, or under a

sleeping spell. The cut is smooth, not ragged as it would be if she was struggling, and there is no bruising under the restraint marks."

Simon leaned on the table gripping its edge to steady himself.

Liam touched his arm. "Sorry, Sarge," he said softly. "We've been at this all night. I guess I forgot she was just a little girl."

"We'll get them, Liam." Simon squared his shoulders. "You and Evarts find something I can use, and we'll get them."

CHAPTER SEVEN

Simon caught a nap on the couch in his office, awakening to the sound of Jack and Liam talking as they entered the room.

"I'm sure I've seen that sigil before," Liam was saying. "Somewhere out Lantilling way, back when I worked for the Border Guard."

"That's as may be," Jack replied. "And Froncek says it could be the one he saw on the sledge last night. But that don't mean it has anything to do with the dead kids. Not saying you're wrong, but Simon'll want more confirmation before we go haring off to the Borderlands.

"But what would a sledge from near the Borderlands be doing in the Hollows?" Liam persisted.

Simon sat up and looked at the timepiece on the wall. It was almost sixteenth hour. He'd slept longer than he'd intended.

"The linen supply company is based out of West Faring."

Jack entered, speaking to Liam over his shoulder. "And yes, I know that's only a few leagues from the border."

Liam followed Jack in and noticed Simon sitting on the couch, rubbing his eyes. "Oh, sorry Sarge. Did we wake you?"

Jack grinned; the first time Simon had seen him smile in weeks. "Catching a few snores, Boss? That couch will wreck your back."

Simon stood and stretched. "I was tired enough to sleep on a rock pile. What's got you in such a good mood?"

"That tailor, Froncek, picked one of the sigils out of the book Lt. Lillihammer gave us as maybe the one he saw last night. It's registered to an Elf-owned linen supply outfit named Silverlake and Company. Their office is in West Faring, out near the border.

"All good," said Simon. "Is there any connection to Hiramis Silverlake?"

"There must be," Liam insisted

Simon drummed his fingers on the desk "It's suggestive, I agree. But Silverlake isn't an unusual name and a lot of Elves, especially from the Free People, own businesses in the Commonwealth. Besides, Silverlake's school is in the Northwest, not West Faring."

"So you think it's just a coincidence?" Liam asked.

"Or not. Until we run a background check on Silverlake, and get more information on the linen company, we won't know."

"The clothing the children wore had laundry marks etched into the weave. Kyle brought it out with a Reveal and got this." Liam showed Simon an image that he'd stored to his handheld mirror, the outline of a pair of crossed hammers. "Show Simon the sigil that Froncek identified," he told Jack.

Jack held out the image printed in black and gray on a sheet of copy paper. It showed crossed hammers surrounded by a circle of Elfscript: *Silverlake and Company Linen.*

"So it's a bit more than suggestive,. But likely not enough for a Justice to issue a warrant without corroboration." Simon sat behind the desk and motioned Jack and Liam to sit on the couch. "What's your take, Jack?"

Again the rare smile. "I think he's on to something, but I've learned to pass this sort of thing up the line and let the Sergeants and Lieutenants deal with it. And even if Liam's right, we need some other corroboration. We don't even know if this linen company had a sledge in the area last night. So what if the two Silverlakes are connected? With the only witness a drunken Orc, we won't get a hearing from a Justice."

"Why? Because the witness was drunk? Or because he was an Orc?" asked Liam.

Jack frowned. "What are you saying, Aster? You think I got something against Orcs?"

"If the boot fits the foot," said Liam. "Everybody knows Orcs aren't reliable, right?"

Jack came up off the couch and faced Liam who also stood, glaring down at the angry Dwarf.

"I'll not have any man say I'm down on a fellow Keeper. D'ye hear?" said Jack through clenched teeth.

"You're the one who brought that up." Liam bristled. "I never mentioned it."

"No, but you've been dancing around it for a week now," Jack retorted. "I told Hal and I'll tell you. It ain't that he's an Orc. It's that he ain't Ham."

Simon stepped between them. "That's enough, both of you. We have a case and we'll work it as a team, or by the gods I'll transfer the lot of you and start over from scratch."

Liam slumped back onto the couch. "Sorry, Jack, I was out of line."

Jack grunted. He rolled his shoulders as if working out a kink and rubbed a hand across his face. "All good," he said. "Don't mean nothing." He sat back down and looked at Simon, his expression all business again. "Do you want me to lean on Froncek, Sarge? Get a more positive identification?"

Simon considered that option for a moment "No, that won't help. You'll only compromise his testimony if we ever need it. And things are shaky enough down in the Hollows without adding Keeper harassment to the mix."

"Harassment? What did I miss?" asked Hal as he entered. He cocked his head at Liam who gave him a thin smile and made room for him on the couch. Only then did Simon notice Kermal standing shyly in the door. He wondered how much the Half -Orc had heard.

"We may have a lead on the sledge that the tailor saw, but nothing yet to tie it to the dead children." Simon quickly related Jack and Liam's findings.

"Well, for what it's worth, Hiramis Silverlake seems to be on the straight," said Hal. "He's been running the school called the Cloister for the past seven years, all registered and proper according to the King's Education Ministry."

"Background?" Simon asked.

"Good family, from the Free People out of Nordale in the far Northwest." Hal checked a small notebook. "Educated at King Olaf University; no criminal record. Looks clean as a mountain spring."

"Any connection to this Silverlake and Company?" asked Liam.

Hal slapped the notebook closed. "It's a big family. Could be, but nothing direct that I came across."

Kermal stepped into the room and stood next to Hal. Liam looked a bit guilty but smiled at the armorer amiably. Jack nodded in greeting as well but said nothing.

"Brackenville here has some new information as well, don't you lad?" said Hal, a bit too cheerfully.

Simon sighed inwardly. *At least he's trying.*

Kermal kept his eyes on Hal as he answered. "I found that craftsman near All God's Square. He's a Southron who makes most of the clan totems and head dresses for all the

Azeri clans in Cymbeline. Actually his shop does. He has a dozen workers who do most of the actual crafting. The shop made half a dozen Oxtail headdresses over the past month, mostly for locals, but two were mail orders. He remembered that because one was ordered from Fastnet, way up in the Northwest."

"Silverlake's school in near enough to Fastnet as makes no difference," said Hal.

"All good," said Simon. "Hal, I want you and Jack to check out that linen company and see if there's any connection to Hiramis Silverlake. Maybe the school uses their linen? See if they had a sledge in the city in the past few days. If we put that together with Froncek's identification, we should be able to talk a Justice into a warrant to search their sledges for trace."

Hal glanced at Jack who sat with arms crossed still staring at the floor "We'll get on it first thing in the morning. Hopefully a conversation with their main office out in West Faring will answer both questions. Do you want us to track down Hiramis Silverlake as well?"

"If you can. But we need something that gets us a warrant. That's your priority." Simon turned to Brackenville. "Kermal, get in touch with Lily Ponsaka. She promised to have her cook Ciara available for an interview tomorrow. Ciara came from the Cloister to work for Lily. Find out everything you can about the school. Do they follow the traditions for their students? Could Seri have had a Naming Ceremony there? She may be more willing to talk to you than to me or Liam."

"Understood," said Kermal.

Simon thought he detected a hint of reluctance in the response. *Or maybe he thinks I'm basing his assignment on his race. I am, but the fact is, he's also the best person for the job. He'll have to understand that.* "Liam," he continued, "can you think of any other avenues to figure out what type of Blood spell the children were used for?"

"Perhaps. I want to reach out to Gran Swampwater down on the Southern Rez. She knows more about Blood magic than anyone. She may be able to give us a lead."

"Good idea," Simon agreed. "See if she'll talk to us."

Liam glanced sideways at Kermal and cleared his throat. "I'd like to take Kermal with me."

Kermal paled. "But, I have to interview the cook." He cast an appealing look at Simon.

"I'm sure Liam can accommodate you. It may be better to wait until later in the morning for the traffic to thin out on the S393. Things always jam up around Bowater until after eighth hour or so."

"But . . ." Kermal swallowed hard then sighed. "Yes, sir."

"All good then, everyone?" Simon asked. The team responded with 'ayes' and grunts of affirmation. "Go home and rest. We had a long day and we'll start fresh in the morning. Anyone who has a new idea, send me a message on my mirror. I'm going home."

The rest of the team filed out of the small office. Kermal hung back and caught Simon's eye.

"Something on your mind, Kermal?" Simon asked.

"Yes, s – Sarge," the Half-Orc stammered. "I'm not sure it would be a good idea for me to go with Liam to the Reservation. I'm Southron, Wind Clan. I don't think I'd be very welcome in a Spirit House of the Earth Clan. There's a long history of, well, tension I guess you'd call it, between Wind Clan and the Earth shamans."

"Whatever your roots, you're half Human, and a Peacekeeper. That alone should make your race irrelevant, at least under the Law. Gran Swampwater may not like you, but if Liam's with you, there won't be trouble."

"If you say so." Kermal didn't sound convinced. "Why did he want me along in the first place?"

"I don't know," said Simon. "Maybe you should ask him. For what it's worth, I think it's a good idea. It's a signal that the King's Peacekeepers are taking the deaths of Orc children seriously."

Kermal looked away. "So you send the token Half-Orc along to make it look like you care."

Simon controlled a flash of anger at the assertion. "You could say that. It's not the real reason, but there's some truth in that ore. You can learn from Liam, and I want your impressions of Gran Swampwater. As you say, she's not Azeri. But talking to Orcs is always hard for Humans. The culture is just different. You know that culture. You may hear things that we miss."

"We?"

"I'll be going with you. Until the Palace answers my request for an interview with the Princess, I haven't got any new leads to follow. Summon me when you finish with the cook and Liam and I will swing by and pick you up on our way south."

CHAPTER EIGHT

By seventh hour the next day, Simon had sent off a formal request for an interview with the Crown Princess, reviewed the Civil Patrol reports from the crime scene, and read Evarts final forensic report on the dead children. All of it added nothing to what he already knew or surmised.

His sleep the night before had been troubled by dreams of dead children that somehow involved Sylvie as well, as if she represented some key to the reason behind the Blood spell that had killed them.

He trusted these types of dreams, vague as they were. Ever since the death of Alira Autumnfall, the Elf woman to whom he'd been engaged before he met Sylvie, his dreams had sometimes foretold events or warned him of possible dangers. He'd always thought they were just the products of his own speculations and feelings. Sylvie was convinced that Alira had imbued him with part of herself, her *ghiras* or higher self as she called it. Simon doubted it, but had to admit that sometimes it seemed that Alira was speaking to him through the dream. Lately, he'd felt Sylvie's presence, as well.

Liam arrived as Simon was perusing Evarts' report for the third time. "G'meeting, Simon," the young mage said as he settled onto the battered couch. "I went over some of my old class notes from the Academy last night and may have a lead on that Blood spell."

Simon put aside the report and waited for Liam to continue.

"Like I said, one of my instructors mentioned a family of Fire based Blood spells. Most Blood magic is Earth, but spells affecting the life force are Fire. That would fit with the findings of Kyle's Reveal spells on the kid's bodies. I don't have any specific notes on what sorts of spells they are, only a general idea of what they affect. I'm hoping Gran Swampwater will know more. At least I have a starting point to ask her about."

"What about the library at Caledonia University? Would they have more information?"

Liam frowned. "Likely, but it would be in the restricted access section. I could get a warrant to look there, but that would take time. I'm betting Gran will have better and more practical information, anyway."

The message tone on Simon's mirror chimed. He glanced at it. "That's Kermal. He's at Lily's getting ready to interview the cook, Ciara. Says we should pick him up in about an hour."

Liam glanced at the timepiece on the wall. "That should get us to Bowater at about ninth hour. Traffic ought to have thinned out by then. We'll make the Rez before midday. I summoned Marshall Greenmire last evening and told him we were coming. He wouldn't guarantee Gran Swampwater would see us, but I made sure he knew this was about Orc children and Blood magic. I'm pretty sure Gran will be willing to talk to us."

Greenmire was the Commonwealth Marshall with jurisdiction over the Southern Reservation. His Southron Azeri heritage didn't seem to get in the way of his duties, but Simon knew he both respected and feared Gran Swampwater as the real authority down there. *All the more reason to take Kermal with us. Maybe he can talk to Greenmire and find out why everyone on the Rez defers to the crones of the Spirit House.*

At half past eighth hour, Simon pulled the four-seat Peacekeeper patrol sled he'd drawn for the day up to the curb in front of Lily's tavern. Kermal got in, taking the rear seat behind Liam.

"What about your flyer?" Liam asked him.

"Lily had her barman stow it in the shed out back. She says it'll be safe there."

Simon pulled the sled away from the curb as Liam and Kermal chatted about the latest model of single seat McGill flyer and its superiority to the Fingal that had been all the rage last year. He waited until they reached the southbound S393 before asking Kermal about his interview with Ciara.

"She didn't want to talk at first," Kermal replied. "I started off by just asking general questions about her work, and how she'd learned about cookery at the Cloisters. She's a bit older than I expected, near on two and twenty, and didn't go to the school until she was fifteen."

"I got the impression from Lily that most of the kids at that school were younger." Simon glanced at him in the rearview.

"That's true. Some older ones do get in, and some stay on to work or teach even as adults. Ciara spent a lot of time on the street before she found her way to the Cloister. She didn't want to speak of that at first, but eventually told me she'd been forced to work in a Scalper brothel from the time she was thirteen. Nose Kronska himself got her out and sent her to the school. He cleared out all the underage girls from the brothels when he took over the gang."

Simon was not surprised Kronska had done that. For a murderous gangster, he had a code of sorts and Simon could believe that it wouldn't allow him to exploit children. *Women over the age of consent, yes, but not children.*

"Ciara said the school was the best thing that ever happened to her," Kermal continued. "And yet there was something about the way she said it that made me think she was glad to be away from it. She wouldn't say anything specific, though. She did say that the blue smocks the dead children wore were the same type that everyone wore at the Cloister." To Liam's inquiring look he said, "She was the one who found them that night, don't you see?"

"Would the school have held a Name Day Ceremony for Seri?" Liam asked.

"Oh, yes. Ciara said they did that sort of thing all the time. The school tries to keep the students grounded in their own culture, the ones who stay there, that is."

"And many don't?" asked Simon.

"That's where Ciara seems to know more than she'll say. She hinted that some of the youngest ones didn't stay very long, which seems strange since you'd think that the older kids would be more likely to run off. I pressed her several times but she just shut down. She repeated that the school had been good to her and she wouldn't say anything more about it."

"Is she hiding something?"

Kermal thought for a second before answering "I couldn't tell if she doesn't know anything for certain, or if she does and is afraid to speak of it."

"I think our next trip will need to be to Fastnet to see this school for ourselves," said Simon. "Hopefully Hal and Jack will dig up enough for a warrant to search that linen company for trace. It looks like there's at least a business connection between them and the Cloister. Maybe a family one as well."

They passed the Bowater ring road in moderate traffic

before ninth hour and Simon increased their speed along the southbound highway. Just outside of the small farming town of Fernhill, Simon took the turnoff for the Reservation. About a mile before they reached the fence, the sled glided past a scorched patch of dried grass and scrub brush.

That's the spot where they ambushed Ham. Simon glanced at Liam but the young mage stared straight ahead, his face set. *There's nothing to mark it, other than that scorched grass, and come spring, even that will turn green. Maybe that's best. Then we can all move on.*

As Liam had predicted, they reached the Reservation gate a few minutes before midday. Marshall Greenmire greeted them at the gatehouse and escorted them to the Administration Center.

"Good meeting, Marshall," said Simon as they climbed out of the sled.

"Sergeant Buckley, Aster, good meeting," Greenmire greeted each of them. He looked Kermal over. "And who might this be?"

"I am Kermal Brackenville, son of Hasfal, born for Wind Clan by Sheila, daughter of George Willows."

"Yondell Greenmire, son of Rigel, born for Wolf Clan by Gretl, daughter of Cord Grassweaver." Greenmire held out a hand and Kermal shook it. "Your mother was Human."

"Aye, she was," said Kermal evenly.

"No disrespect, friend. It's just not common here on the Rez."

Simon spoke up in the awkward silence that followed. "Has Gran Swampwater agreed to see us?"

"Aye, she has." Greenmire pointed at Kermal. "She especially said I was to bring the Orc Keeper to her."

Kermal paled but said nothing.

"Lead on, then," said Liam.

They left their sidearms and Simon's Reaper locked in the rear compartment of their sled. All outside spells were forbidden within two *li,* about two hundred yards, of the

Spirit House.

The Spirit House was a low walled compound built of mud bricks and living trees. The corner pillars were live oaks, the doorframes and lintels flowering dogwoods. Windows were unglazed but screened by intertwined willow shoots. Two crones met them at the entrance. Simon wasn't sure if they were the same old Orc women who had greeted them the last time he'd been here. It likely didn't matter. They showed no sign of recognition, but pointed their short staves of intertwined oak and iron at Greenmire.

"You are granted entry to the House of the Earth Spirit. Will you enter willingly and abide by the laws of this place?" Greenmire spoke in a deep and formal tone.

Simon took a step forward and bowed to the crones. "We will."

One of the old women pointed her staff at Brackenville. "You are scion of the Wind Spirit," she said harshly. "Will you give your bond to abide by the laws of this place?"

Before Simon could speak up and say that as a Peacekeeper, Brackenville was under his command, Kermal stepped in front of him.

"I so give my bond on the honor of my father, and the *strahk* of the Wind," he said. "But I am a sworn officer of the King's Justice. That alone should be bond enough."

The crone let out a short cackling laugh. "Your King has no writ in this House, young Orc. Be at peace and enter."

The two crones led them across the open center of the compound and down a short passage formed by willow branches that arched overhead to intertwine in a solid roof. It ended at the entrance to an earthen room illuminated by several skylights of thick commercial grade glass. Soft Glenharrow wool rugs covered the floor. A round table and six chairs dominated the center of the room. A small FarSpeaker in one corner played soft Elven dulcimer music and a copper kettle bubbled on an ordinary Fire spell salamander.

Simon looked around, puzzled by the modern furnishings.

CHAPTER NINE

"You are surprised, Simon Buckley of the Fire Spirit?" asked a mellow voice from behind him. "Would you begrudge an old woman a few comforts?"

Simon turned and bowed to Olega Swampwater. She was old and weathered but stood tall, almost as tall as Simon himself and her voice was that of a much younger woman. Now, it held a touch of gentle humor and good-natured teasing in its round tone. She wore a simple gown woven of soft wool, but she still held the long ebony staff tipped with polished onyx that signified her status as Gran, Revered Mother of the Sprit House.

"I mean no disrespect," Simon answered. "But I am surprised. Commercial spells are forbidden in the Spirit House, are they not?

"I cannot appreciate a comfortable chair and a cup of hot tea?" she asked with a smile. "We are not so backward here at the Spirit House that we don't take advantage of the things the outside world can offer."

Simon blushed and realized that she was gently mocking him for his preconceptions of her and her sisters. "As I said, I mean no disrespect."

She laughed. "Don't be embarrassed, dear boy. I know you are here on serious business. I should not make fun of you." She waved an arm to encompass the entire group. "Sit, all of you. Qunella will pour tea and you can tell me what brings you to my House."

Still blushing, Simon took the nearest chair. Liam sat next to him, grinning, Simon supposed, at Gran's teasing. Kermal sat across from Gran, facing the door and as far away from her as possible across the small table. Gran appeared not to notice.

One of the crones who had been guarding the door took the bubbling kettle from the salamander and quietly made tea, which she poured into earthenware cups. She set a cup before each of them, placed the kettle on a trivet in the middle of the table, then bowed to Gran Swampwater and left the room. The scent of fresh tea seasoned with cardamom filled the room.

Gran Swampwater lifted her cup, sipped, and sighed. "Qunella does make a very good cup of tea.". She looked at Simon. "You are troubled, Simon Buckley. And you have come to me. Do your concerns involve my people, or is this a matter of Blood?"

"Perhaps both, Gran." Simon sipped his tea, considering how to proceed. "Two days ago, the bodies of four Orc children, all around ten years of age, were found in a vacant lot behind a tavern in the Hollows in Cymbeline. Many of your people have ended up in that part of the city, and while two of the children were definitely Azeri, the other two may have been of yours."

"Dead children are tragic wherever they come from, but that is not why you seek my help. These children, I surmise, did not meet the God of Death through natural means?

"No." Simon shook his head. "The children were positioned in a neat row with obvious care, and had been killed elsewhere before being brought to the place where they were found." Simon took a deep swallow of his tea. "Their throats had been cut in a ritual fashion, a Blood ritual."

"Do you know what sort of Blood spell or curse was powered by their life energy?" Gran asked, looking into her cup.

"Not specifically," Liam said. "I was able to determine that it was a Fire spell of some sort. The troubling thing is that it seems to have completely drained all trace of life from them. There is no residual aura, no life energy at all in any of the bodies."

Gran exhaled with a slight hiss. "So, the rumors are true."

"Rumors?" asked Simon.

Gran looked up from her tea. "I once told Sylvie Graystorm that *ghiras* mattered more than blood. *Ghiras* is the life force that flows from the *strahk* of every living thing. *Ghiras* is the aura that you humans analyze and trap with your forensic spells. It touches every spell a mage casts, making it unique to the caster. But your understanding of it is imperfect. You believe that is fixed to the body and drains away after death at a predicable rate."

"And that isn't true?" asked Liam. "Our algorithms and formulas seem to work pretty well based on that understanding."

Gran smiled. "For the most part. But *ghiras* is intertwined with *strahk,* stronger when the individual is attuned to the *strahk* of their birth spirit, weaker when not. The longer we live, the less attuned we become but the more tightly our *ghiras* is bound to the body. That is why your algorithms work. In children, *ghiras* can be especially strong, but weakly held to the body."

"What has that to do with the dead children?" Liam

persisted. "The aura, the *ghiras* as you call it, was completely gone. How is that possible?"

"You found the traces of the Fire spell," said Gran. "What did you learn about Blood powered Fire spells from your mentors?"

"Only that they affected the life force but weren't practical since they drained life from the caster."

Gran folded her hands. "True, as far as they told you. But we know of a way that with Blood and Fire, a *ghiras* that is weakly bound to a body can be made to flow into another with caster as the medium through which it flows. Some of the caster's life is drained, but if that life is very strong, or very ancient, it has *ghiras* to spare."

Simon struggled to digest what she had just said. "You mean, these children were sacrificed so that their life could be transferred to another person?"

"I fear that may be so," said Gran. "We have heard rumors of missing children, young ones taken for dark rituals somewhere in the Borderlands of the Havens." She shook her head. "Such tales are common, usually aimed at a particular Elf Lord with disputed holdings or with a reputation for mistreating the Orcs who labor for the Lord's estates. No one believed such stories. But lately they have been told in earnest, not about a particular Lord, but as a dark secret with real power behind it."

"Who could confirm if there is any truth to these rumors?" asked Simon.

"No one here," Gran answered. "Perhaps you should ask your armorer."

Kermal jumped as if she had poked him. "Me? What would I know?"

"You are the son of Hasfal Brackenville are you not?'

"My father left that life when he married my mother. He was shunned by the Cabal until the day he died."

"The name Brackenville will still command attention in the Cabal of Clans." Gran held her hand out toward Kermal, palm up, thumb and forefinger touching. "*Kul ghiras annan sarngal.*"

Kermal leaped up, almost knocking over his chair. "Save your spells, Witch. I don't believe in your '*ghiras* follows the Blood' curses. I'm a King's Peacekeeper, not some Orc shaman terrorizing his own people into submission."

"Agent Brackenville," Simon said sharply. "We are guests in this House."

Kermal reddened. He took a deep breath and bowed his head. "My apologies, Gran Swampwater. I gave my bond." He turned to Simon and said, "I'll be in the Administration Center, sir. I'm sorry, but I can't continue here."

"We'll discus that later," said Simon. "You're dismissed, Agent."

Kermal bowed to Gran Swampwater and left the room without another word.

"I apologize for my Agent, Gran—"

"No," Gran interrupted. "He is young and trying to balance between two worlds. I should apologize for calling him out."

"What does his father have to do with our case?" Liam asked.

"It's not my place to explain." Gran smoothed her skirts. "If Kermal Brackenville is willing, he will tell you himself. But only he can take you to those who may know the truth. I fear your four dead children are only a small part of the story."

"This Blood spell you spoke of," said Liam. "What does it require? Why children?"

"I don't have answers for you, Liam Aster. I only know that the spell exists and that the Blood of a sentient combines with Fire to cast it. The details are forgotten. We forbade such magic long before your Commonwealth existed."

Simon waited for Gran to elaborate or explain more about Kermal. She knew far more than she seemed willing to say but he couldn't think of a way to approach her. He had heard of the Cabal. Every Keeper had. But its existence was usually dismissed as a myth, or at most a collection of unrelated stories attributed to a mysterious shadow group. None of his superiors took it seriously. Clearly, Gran Swampwater did; maybe Kermal as well.

Gran deflected any further questions politely but firmly. It was clear that the interview was over.

Simon stood and bowed deeply. "Thank you for meeting with us, Gran Swampwater. Good parting."

"Good parting, Simon Buckley of the Fire Spirit. And convey my blessing to Sylvie Graystorm. I read her *ghiras* in your eyes and I'm glad that she has found so worthy a match."

Simon jerked his head up at the mention of Sylvie. *How does Gran know about us? And what does she mean 'read her ghiras in my eyes'?*

Before he could ask any questions, Gran inclined her head slightly before turning and leaving the room.

They rode back to Cymbeline in silence after retrieving Kermal at the Administration Center. He had climbed into the sled's rear seat without a word to Simon or Liam. Liam drove and Simon glanced back occasionally in a silent invitation for Kermal to talk, but the Half-Orc said nothing, staring at the passing landscape.

Liam pulled to the curb outside Lily's place just before sixteenth hour and Simon climbed out with Kermal, signaling to Liam to remain in the sled.

Kermal looked at Simon. "I know. I made a mess of the meeting. But I told you it wasn't a good idea for me to be there."

"You were there under my orders and I expected you to act like a Peacekeeper." Simon told him. "I won't ask you explain your behavior at the Spirit House. Put it down to an Orc thing that I can't understand. But I will ask what Gran Swampwater meant when she suggested you could lead us to some answers about these children."

Kermal looked away and sighed. "My father was once an enforcer for the Cabal. He did a lot of things he refused to talk about when he was alive. For most of my life, I believed he was just a meat packer in the stockyard by our house. We lived in the East End, don't you see. Both my mother's family and the Wind Clan shunned us. But every month or two, some Orc would knock at the door and ask for my father. Sometimes he'd send them away, other times he'd listen to them for a few minutes and then tell my mother he was going out for a drink. She always locked the door after he left and sent me to my room and told me not to come out until she said to. I found out after he died that he still did jobs for the Cabal, if the need was great enough."

"Holy Mother of All, Kermal. You didn't think to mention this? How in the Hells did you pass the Security screen for the Academy?"

"It never came up," said Kermal. "No one but the Cabal knew what my father really was. And he was very good at it. He never left any witnesses." He paused for a moment. "Consider that, Sarge. My father killed people. He wasn't above killing innocents who happened to see his face. And yet he never showed that side to my mother and me. With us, he was always gentle and patient. Even when I pushed him to the point where I could tell he wanted to beat the shit out of me, he never did. He never raised a hand to my mother. Or me."

"He must have loved you both," said Simon.

"That's not my point, Simon." Kermit's voice was a low growl. "When I found out who he really was, I couldn't believe it. I was sixteen at the time, just when a young man realizes his father isn't the hero of his childhood. Can you imagine what that does to a person? To find out that the man who raised you, who tucked you into bed every night, was a cold-blooded murderer. His name was a curse and a legend to the enemies of the Cabal, and I never knew who he really was."

"And that's what Gran Swampwater meant when she said that your name still carried weight with the Cabal?" Simon kept his tone even.

Kermal looked away again. "I suppose so. But I never had any contact with them. It's probably why I became a Peacekeeper. When I found out what he'd done all his life, I wanted to put myself as far from that as I could."

"Why does Gran think the Cabal has information about these children?" Simon asked.

"I don't know that, Simon. Hand to the gods, I don't know. The Cabal isn't just a bunch of old Orcs sitting around playing tiles and reliving the old days. They're dangerous people and they don't tolerate questions, especially from the King's Peacekeepers. If they know who killed these kids, they either sanctioned it or they will deal with it through the Clans."

Simon closed his eyes and took a deep breath. It was a lot to take in. The Cabal was real, or at least it was real to Gran Swampwater, and to Kermal. All his professional life he'd thought of the Cabal as a fiction, a legend used to frighten children and new Keepers. *To think that it's real and could wield real power is hard to believe.* "I won't ask you to do anything, now." He looked Kermal in the eye. "But if the time came when I needed to speak to them, is Gran right? Could you make that happen?"

Kermal exhaled and looked at the sky. "I know a man, someone my father knew from before I was born. He was at my father's death rites and gave me a mirror locus to call if I needed anything." He looked at Simon. "I told him I would never call. That I knew what my father had done and I wanted none of it."

"What did he say?" asked Simon, catching the look of fear in Kermal's face.

"*Kul ghiras annan sarngal.* Spirit follows the Blood. It's supposedly the oath of the Cabal."

Simon and Liam left Kermal at the tavern to retrieve his flyer. Simon hadn't pressed the armorer further. The case was already a tangled mess without introducing more complications. He hoped Hal and Jack had been able to get a lead from the linen company, because other than Gran Swampwater's cryptic allusion to some sort of life-transferring Blood spell, this whole morning had yielded nothing but new questions. The rumors of other missing children didn't surprise him, but right now, the only children he knew about for certain were the four that had been found in Lily's back lot.

"What did you make of the Blood spell Gran Swampwater mentioned?" he asked Liam as the mage guided the sled up Canal Street toward Wycliffe House.

"It fits what I remembered from the Academy," Liam answered. "But she was pretty vague about the actual mechanics. Orc understanding of how magic works is just different. They rely more on *ghiras* and intuition than quantum principles. It makes it hard to figure out what they're talking about sometimes."

"But children?" asked Simon. "*Ghiras* bound to the body and transference of life force? It sounds like some old grandmothers' tale."

"Like I said, Simon, Orc magic is just different."

Before Simon could reply, the summoning tone on his handheld mirror interrupted. He waved a hand to activate the mirror and Stenson Harold's scarred face swam into view. "Lieutenant Harold. What can I do for you?"

"Good meeting, Sergeant Buckley," said Harold. "The Palace Protocol Office has granted your request for an interview with the Crown Princess."

"That was fast," said Simon.

"The Princess herself took a hand. Apparently she's anxious to talk to you. Be at the South Postern Gate at seventeenth hour today. The guards will clear you in and I'll provide an escort to the meeting room."

"May I bring another Keeper from my team?"

Harold frowned. "Why?"

"Standard protocol," Simon lied. "It's either that or a recording mirror to corroborate any leads we develop from the Princess's information."

"One other man," agreed Harold. "I'll inform the guard Captain."

"Thank you, Lieutenant," said Simon. Harold nodded and broke the spell with a wave of his hand. Simon stared at his blank mirror for a second before looking at Liam.

"What was that dreck about standard protocol needing two Keepers for an interview?" Liam asked.

Simon grinned at him. "How else was I going to get you in?"

"Me?"

"Yes. I want you there to give me your impressions of the Princess."

"Why?"

"Because she's either a Fire mage herself and the rest of the world doesn't know it, or she's a Latent and possibly very dangerous."

CHAPTER TEN

Despite late afternoon traffic, they arrived at the Palace a few minutes before seventeenth hour. The South Postern Gate faced King's Road and was the main business entrance to the Royal compound. Unlike the gilded and filigreed Gryphon Gate, where public appearances by the King and Royal family were staged, this was where the real business of the Palace took place. Liam steered the sled slowly through the zigzag maze of stone and concrete security barriers up to the guard kiosk next to the iron gate.

A guardsman in a green and gold doublet stepped out of the kiosk. He held a D'Stang heavy bolt thrower at port arms and Simon noted the bulge of tactical body armor under the Royal livery.

"Names," the guardsman said.

Simon held up his Peacekeeper badge. "Sergeant Simon Buckley, Magic Enforcement. This is Agent Liam Aster, King's Peacekeepers. Lieutenant Harold should have cleared us."

The guardsman examined their badges, spoke into a FarSpeaker bracer on his wrist and then waved Liam through the gate. "Park the sled there." He indicated an alcove to the left of the guard post. "Do not leave the vehicle until an escort arrives. All weapons, blades, and spell components must remain in the sled. There are security spells on every door, so don't attempt to disregard these restrictions. Understood?"

"Aye, sir," answered Liam. "Why the heightened security?"

"Just park the sled over there, Agent."

Liam swung the sled into the spot indicated by the guardsman. A few minutes later, Lt. Harold approached them. Simon leaned against the sled, waiting.

"Good meeting, Sergeant Buckley," said Harold. "The Princess is waiting."

"Good meeting, Lieutenant Harold," replied Simon.

Harold pointed across the alcove. "This way."

Simon walked next to Harold and Liam fell in behind him. Harold led them through a narrow passage and up a winding stone stairway. A heavy wooden door at the top opened onto a long gallery with high windows overlooking King's Road. Below them, Simon noticed that a pair of armored personnel sledges had moved in and parked next to the security barriers. "Why the increased security?" he asked as their footsteps rang on the polished wooden floor of the gallery.

"You mean aside from the latest coup in the Azeri Empire?"

Simon smiled. "So who's on top this week?"

Harold laughed. "Point taken. No, we don't usually care about which warlord manages to grab the crown. But this time, the intelligence mavens think it may signal an increased threat level. That, and the fires."

"Fires?"

Harold's demeanor grew guarded. "There have been some fires around the Palace grounds. Mostly minor and not near the living quarters, but the Fire Marshal says they were arson. It's got the King on edge, so we're all on alert."

"Was the Princess in the Palace when these fires started?" asked Simon.

Harold arched an eyebrow. "Now why would you ask that?"

"Curiosity."

"More than that, I think."

Simon glanced sidelong at Harold. The security officer's scarred face might have been carved from oak. "I saw what happened at Lily's with the towels."

The side of Harold's mouth twitched upward in a tiny smile, or perhaps a grimace. "You mean the towels that fell onto a hot stove and caught fire?"

He knows something, Simon thought. "Is that what happened?"

"Isn't it?" Harold smiled more broadly as they reached the tall door at the end of the gallery. He gestured toward it. "The Princess is waiting."

Harold opened the door and stood aside as Simon and Liam entered, followed them in and closed the door behind them. Simon took in the room, a library from the look of it with floor to ceiling bookshelves. Several heavy oak desks littered with more books and papers surrounded a cluster of overstuffed chairs covered in gold brocade. Between two of the chairs a low glass-topped serving table with legs carved into coiled dragons was set with a gold tea service.

Princess Rebeka sat in a high-backed armchair facing the door. She was dressed in a business suit of dark green cloth offset by a gold scarf, a not too subtle invocation of the Royal colors, and her hair was pulled up in a loose bun. Her green eyes looked even brighter next to the dark cloth of her jacket. She wore a thin gold chain hung with a faceted blue stone around her neck and when she moved to face them a pair of polished wooden bracelets slid down to her right wrist from under her jacket. Simon glanced at Liam who was watching the princess with narrowed eyes.

On the chair to Rebeka's left sat an Elf. He was dark haired with the violet eyes and smaller ears of the Free People. He wore a modern business suit of dark blue breeches and jacket, white hose and shirt with a red cravat; every inch the modern Commonwealth businessman. He sat still in the chair, but his hands never stopped moving, straightening his already straight cravat, tugging at his cuffs, pulling at his hose.

He's trying to look calm, but something is making him nervous. Us? The Elf glanced quickly, almost imperceptibly at Rebeka. *The Princess?*

Harold moved up to Simon's side and announced, "Sergeant Buckley, Your Highness."

Simon drew himself up to attention and executed a passable formal bow. Liam did the same. "Thank you for receiving us, Your Highness."

Rebeka gave a wry laugh "Did I really have a choice, Sergeant? I'm sure you would have approached the King's Prosecutor next, even at the cost of your own career."

Simon smiled slightly, knowing she was right. He bowed his head in her direction. "As you say, Princess."

Her eyes narrowed for a moment before she turned to Liam. "And who might this be?"

Before Simon could speak, Liam stepped forward and bowed deeply. "King's Agent Liam Aster, Your Highness." He lifted her hand as he bowed over it and barely touched it with his lips. He straightened but held her eye.

Rebeka stared at him for a second, a deep blush coloring her fair skin. She swallowed hard. "Yes, I see," she stammered. "Please, both of you sit. You, too, Stenson."

After they were seated, she seemed to regain her composure. She gestured to the Elf at her left. "This is . . ."

"Hiramis Silverlake, I presume," interrupted Simon. It

was rude, he knew, but he wanted to keep both the Princess and this Elf of hers off balance.

The Elf jerked his head slightly, glanced once again at Rebeka, then composed himself. "Yes, Sergeant. I am Hiramis Silverlake."

"Lily Ponsaka sends her regards," said Simon. The mention of Lily seemed to make Silverlake more uncomfortable. Simon glanced at Rebeka, but the Princess's expression remained cool and unperturbed. "She's been trying to reach you for some time now," Simon continued. "But your staff didn't seem to know your whereabouts."

"I was traveling." Silverlake picked at the hem of his sleeve. "Soliciting donors is a distasteful but necessary part of my duties. The staff is perfectly capable of running the school in my absence."

"So your staff would know when and how Jochim and Seri Marshstrider and two other young children left your school and found their way to a vacant lot here in the capitol," Simon pushed, trying to keep Silverlake on the defensive.

Silverlake shook his head, but wouldn't meet Simon's eye. "Our children are carefully monitored and protected. No one would allow a young child to simply leave the compound."

"And yet, four children from your school were found dead in a vacant lot here in Cymbeline. How did that happen?"

"Tell them Hiramis," said Rebeka in a tone so cold and harsh that Simon turned to look at her.

"He assured me that it was a legitimate apprenticeship," protested Silverlake. "The children would be cared for, given work and shelter by his *Syr,* and eventually have an opportunity to have their own plot to farm."

"Tell him everything, Hiramis." Rebeka's eyes narrowed and her hands gripped the arms of her chair.

Silverlake reddened and a thin sheen of sweat began to gleam on his forehead. He pulled at his cravat. "You must understand, we have no King's School certification. We depend on contributions from donors and on what our students can earn in order to continue our work. Of late, money has been even scarcer than in the past and the need has increased month-by-month; so many young ones in need. It was a question of turning more children away, or even closing down some of the dormitories. I had no other options." He glanced at Rebeka who glared back at him.

"What are you trying to say, Mr. Silverlake?" asked Simon. "Did you take money for sending these children to another institution?"

"He sold them," said Rebeka in a low, flat tone. "He sent them into virtual slavery in the Havens."

"No, Your Highness, please," whined the Elf. "It wasn't like that. We were desperate. He offered enough money to keep the doors open for three months. It was only the four children, all of them young, fresh from the streets. They hadn't grown accustomed to the school routine, hadn't yet grown attached. And it wasn't supposed to be an indenture. They were to be placed with Orc households on the estate. They'd learn farming."

"They'd learn to be field hands," growled Rebeka. "You betrayed them, Hiramis. More importantly, you betrayed me. I lent my name to your school, staked my reputation with Mistress Ponsaka and her people on your word that these children would be safe."

Silverlake writhed in his chair as if in pain as her words lashed him. His face turned bright red and he gasped for breath and ripped his cravat away. Simon began to rise from his chair as an electric tingle ran down his spine. The air around Silverlake shimmered with heat.

Liam leaned forward and gripped Rebeka's right wrist, covering the slim wooden bracelets. She shifted her glare from Silverlake to Liam. He met her eye and shook his head slightly. She covered his hand with her left and pulled at his grip, half rising from her seat. Liam held on and shook his head again.

Rebeka cocked her head as if surprised then exhaled sharply and sank back into the chair, tearing her eyes away from Liam's. Simon felt a sharp ping at the base of his spine and the heat around Silverlake evaporated.

The Elf sank to the floor and sobbed. "I'm sorry, Princess," he choked. "I'm sorry."

Rebeka ignored him. She shrank into the chair, staring at the floor. Liam moved to her side, holding her hands and speaking in a low whisper. Simon could not hear his words, but Rebeka did. She nodded but kept her head bowed.

Harold moved forward, reaching for Liam but stopped when Simon gripped his shoulder.

"She's more a threat to him than he is to her," whispered Simon. "How long have you known?"

"Six months," said Harold. "She didn't dare say anything to the Family, or to the Parliament. The Accords, you know. She'd be stripped of her title and exiled."

Simon understood. Under the Commonwealth Accords that had ended the old Magisterium, no member of the Royal Family could become a mage. The root of the Magisterium's hold on the throne had been the total control of magic by the Family. The magical revolution had broken that monopoly and made it accessible to all, while the Accords had forbidden it to ever again occupy the throne.

Simon caught Liam's eye over the top of Rebeka's head. The young mage cleared his throat and said, "Your Highness, I think you and I should talk in private somewhere else. Would that be all good with you?"

Rebeka looked at Simon, then at Harold. She straightened her back and disengaged her wrists from Liam's grasp.

"Stenson," she said to Harold. "Agent Aster and I will withdraw to the music room."

"But, Your Highness, I can't leave Sergeant Buckley unattended in the library. In fact, both he and Agent Aster are only cleared for accompanied visitor access."

"Oh, for the Gods' sake, Stenson. We'll only be in the next room. You can stay here with the Sergeant if you must."

"But Your Highness," began Harold.

Rebeka's composure cracked. "I don't care about your stupid protocols," she said with a sob. "I need to talk to someone about this, about this thing that I've become. You can't tell me what I should do, and Father will never understand. This man already knows what I am and may be able to help me. Let me do this."

Harold looked at Simon who just shrugged.

"As you say, Your Highness," Harold replied softly. "I'll detail a man to watch the other door. I'll remain here with the Sergeant."

Rebeka gave him a grateful smile and turned away toward a door set into the far wall. Liam followed closely at her side, and resumed speaking softly to her. She cocked her head, listening intently

Simon took Silverlake's right arm and pulled him up from the floor. The Elf got unsteadily to his feet. Simon put a hand on his chest and with a small shove pushed him back into a chair. He put his hands on the arms of the chair and leaned in close to Silverlake's face. "Now, you will give me the name of the person who paid you," he said. "Or I'll call Agent Aster back and allow the Princess to do whatever she wishes with you."

Silverlake looked away, not meeting Simon's hard gaze. "His name is Grimsley, Sailesh Grimsley."

"Human?"

Silverlake slunk lower in his seat. "An Orc. A Hyberian by his accent, I believe. He said he was an Overseer for an Elf Lord from the Borderlands."

"And the Elf Lord's name?"

"I'm not sure. It may be Lindenfield, at least that was the name of the estate he claimed to represent. His sled had a sigil on the door that read Lindenfield Farms. He signed the papers for the children's release in his own name and paid in cash, so I don't know for a certainty."

"What else can you tell me about him? Age, appearance, coloring? Did he pay in Commonwealth crowns or Elfcoin?"

"He was an Orc," whined Silverlake. "They all look alike. He had very pale skin, no scars or tattoos and spoke with a thick Hyberian accent. I could barely understand him. But he paid in new Commonwealth crowns." Silverlake paused and looked thoughtful. "He drove a big Hilten six seat sled and there were already several children in it. I didn't see them clearly, but there were at least three. I asked him about them, but he just grunted at me and said they were orphans from the city. I suppose he meant Cymbeline."

"What were the names of the other two children you sold?" Simon pressed. "We've already identified Jochim and Seri. Who were the other two?"

"They were from the East side of the capitol, orphans I was told. They said very little, but gave their names as Gerling and Astrida Harmish. I think they were brother and sister. They were definitely Azeri."

"Ox clan?" asked Simon.

Silverlake looked puzzled. "Yes. So were Jochim and Seri. How do you know that?"

"How did they come to your school?"

"I don't recall," said Silverlake. "Most of the children from the capitol come through Mistress Ponsaka. Occasionally private agents in other parts of the city contact us. Perhaps the children came through one of them. My staff would know."

"Would Biran Stillwater be one of those 'agents'?" Simon wasn't sure why it occurred to him that Stillwater and the Loblollies might be involved. Something Kermal had said about the Ox clan and children missing from the East End and Nose Kronska mentioning the 'Lollies poaching on Scalper territory out near the stockyards.

Stillwater jerked as if slapped. "How do you know these

things?"

"How many children did Stillwater send you?" demanded Simon. "What happened to them?"

Silverlake glanced at the door to the room where the Princess was still with Liam. He lowered his voice. "Some are still at the school. Most were kept in a separate dormitory for a day or two until Grimsley picked them up. That was the arrangement I had with Stillwater. He paid to house the children and Grimsley paid when the children were picked up. But the last time Grimsley came, we were four children short of what Grimsley said he was promised. He made threats; he could have destroyed everything we'd built. I had no choice."

"You betrayed her trust," said Simon quietly. "You betrayed the trust of those children."

"I have saved hundreds of children from the streets." Silverlake grew defiant. "I did what I had to for the sake of the school. They were supposed to be safe. Yes, in the Havens where their kind has certain disadvantages. But it would still be better than living on the streets."

"But they aren't alive, Mr. Silverlake," Simon again leaned in close to Silverlake, forcing the Elf to meet his eye. "They're dead, laid out like animals in a vacant lot in Cymbeline. How do you think that happened?"

"It wasn't my fault," cried Silverlake, his defiance breaking. "They were all good when they left the school two weeks ago. Whatever happened to them after that is on Grimsley, not me."

"Where do we find Grimsley?" asked Simon, leaning back in his chair. "How does he contact you?"

"He doesn't. I get a message from Stillwater that he has some children to place. I message my cousin, Horace, and within two or three days, Grimsley arrives."

"Horace Silverlake?" Simon asked pointedly. "The linen supplier?"

Silverlake glanced up sharply, confirming Simon's guess

at the cousin's business. "Yes. He gives me a discount on the linens for the school. He also supplies several estates in the Borderlands."

"Lindenfield?" asked Simon.

Silverlake shrank back into the chair. "I don't know. We aren't that close."

Simon turned to Harold. "Is this person under Royal protection?"

Harold shook his head. "Not that I know of. The Princess hasn't told me anything about his disposition."

"Good." Simon took out his handheld mirror and activated the recording spell. "Hiramis Silverlake, I am placing you under lawful detention for the crimes of child endangerment and accessory to kidnap. You are under caution that any statements you make may be recorded and used in evidence against you. You have the right to legal counsel before making any further statements to me or to any other King's Officer. Do you understand?"

Silverlake nodded.

"Please answer for the record." Simon held out the mirror.

"I understand," the Elf said without looking up.

As Simon thumbed the mirror to record his fingerprint as witness, the door to the music room opened and a distressed looking guardsman rushed in.

"Lieutenant," he said to Harold. "The Princess is gone."

"Shit," muttered Harold. To the guard he said, "Search all the adjoining rooms. I'll alert the gate and set Condition 2 throughout the Palace." He glared at Simon then began speaking rapidly through the FarSpeaker bracer at his wrist.

From somewhere deeper in the Palace, a fire alarm began to wail.

CHAPTER ELEVEN

The door to the music room burst open and Rebeka and Liam ran in, the Princess flushed and laughing, Liam smiling.

"Sorry Sarge," Liam said, catching sight of Simon. "Just practicing a basic containment spell. It got away from us and set a few bushes in the Conservatory alight. The extinguisher spells handled it, but I'm afraid Rebeka's mother will need to replace a few rows of shrubbery."

Harold stepped forward, pointed at Liam, and said to the guardsman, "Place this man in restraint until I can get the Master at Arms up here."

"Don't you dare!" Rebeka stepped in front of Liam before the guard could move. "Stenson, stop this nonsense right now. Tell your teams to stand down. I'm not hurt and I won't have Liam, that is Agent Aster, mistreated."

"But your Highness . . ." Harold trailed off when he saw the look on her face, a mixture of rage and fear. He sighed and spoke again into the bracer, "All teams stand down. The Princess is safe. False alarm."

"Thank you, Stenson." The Princess took the older security officer's hand. "I know I'm not easy to guard, but I do know what I'm doing."

"As you say, Princess."

Rebeka turned to Simon. "Did Hiramis answer your questions satisfactorily?"

"Aye, your Highness," said Simon. "But I'm afraid he's now under caution and lawful detention. He'll be leaving with us, unless he's under your protection."

She cocked her head and regarded Simon. "And if I extend him my protection?"

"Then I'll ask Lieutenant Harold to see that he doesn't leave the Palace until I speak to the Kings Prosecutor and get a formal Royal warrant signed by your father."

Rebeka shot a glance at Liam who nodded grimly.

"Hiramis," she said to Silverlake. "You will accompany these Agents to Wycliffe House. If you need counsel, have someone inform me and I'll have George Latham come to you at Wycliffe."

"Yes, Highness." Hiramis gave her a stiff bow.

Simon considered her words. George Latham, of Latham, Ironhelm and Oak, was the preeminent Defense Advocate in the entire Commonwealth. The firm had represented the Royal House in the past. For Rebeka to invoke his name suggested that she had been close indeed to Silverlake.

"What are the charges against him, Sergeant?" Rebeka asked.

"For now, child endangerment and accessory to kidnap."

The Princess frowned. "I understand. Understand me, then. I won't allow anything this man has done to taint the reputation of my House. He has betrayed a trust and what help I offer is for the protection of my name and reputation. Beyond that, do what you must. I want justice for Jochim and Seri. They were the ones who deserved my protection."

She turned to Liam. "May we continue our discussions another time? There's much I need to learn."

"Aye, your Highness. I'm at your disposal anytime I'm not on duty." Liam bowed and kissed her hand again, this time holding it against his lips for a full second. She blushed but did not pull away.

They escorted Silverlake back to the sled by the same route they had taken earlier. Simon and Liam flanked the Elf but hadn't restrained him. Silverlake made no protest and stared dejectedly at his feet as they walked along the gallery. Harold strode ahead of them, grim faced and silent.

Liam tucked Silverlake into the rear seat of the sled and climbed in beside him.

Simon stood by the driver's side door and looked at Harold. "Thank you, Lieutenant Harold. I owe you one."

"Aye, you do," Harold grumbled. "Look to your man, there. I'll not have the Princess hurt."

"Liam is an expert Fire mage, and a good teacher. He won't let the Princess harm herself or others."

"That's not what I meant." Harold cast a sharp look at Liam. "She's over twenty, but still naïve. She's been sheltered all her life."

"You sound like a father, Lieutenant."

"I am. Two daughters, both safely married now. It should be her father talking to Aster. But under the circumstances. " Harold left the sentence hanging and laid a hand on his sidearm.

"Duly noted," said Simon with a smile. "I'll warn Agent Aster."

Simon snapped him a salute, still smiling, and said, "Good parting, Lieutenant."

Harold returned the salute. "Good parting, Buckley." He signaled the guardsman in the gate kiosk before turning on his heel and striding across the courtyard.

Silverlake didn't speak during the ride back to Wycliffe House. Neither did Liam, who spent the trip looking out at the city streets as the sled wove though traffic.

I hope you know what you're getting in to, lad, Simon thought. Training a Royal to be a Fire mage made his own romance with a Gray Ranger look commonplace. And Simon knew firsthand how romantic involvement could hamper an investigation. *This whole thing could fall on us like a rockslide in a coalmine and bury us so deep even Hal couldn't dig us out.*

By the time they had processed Silverlake through Central Booking and seen him led into the cellblocks on the first floor of the House, it was well after twentieth hour of the day. The Elf had remained silent through the whole process other than answering the booking agent's questions about his personal information. Simon wasn't surprised to find Hal waiting for him in the team office.

Simon ran a quick check with the records clerk at Central Booking, and was not surprised to find there was no official record of an Orc named Sailesh Grimsley, at least in the civilian registry. No criminal record, no professional licenses, and especially no record as a sanctioned Overseer.

"Working late again, lad." Hal made it a statement, not a question.

Simon smiled. "We have Hiramis Silverlake in custody."

"So I hear" Hal said. Simon didn't ask how he knew. Hal had been a Keeper for so long that he knew everything that went on in Wycliffe House, usually well before the senior gold-braid types did. "I also hear that George Latham has asked to be endorsed as his advocate. Care to tell me what in the Seven Hells is going on with that?"

Simon leaned back in his chair and crossed his arms. "Lieutenant Harold of Palace Security summoned my mirror just after we dropped Brackenville at Lily's place. The Princess herself cleared us for an interview. Silverlake was with her. He confirmed that he'd acted as go-between for an Orc named Grimsley who has been buying orphans and throwaways from Biran Stillwater and taking them

West to the Havens."

Hal whistled. "And the Princess knew this?"

Simon shook his head. "No, at least she denies it. I believe her. She was royally angry, pardon the pun, when she found out. Almost had Silverlake dead over it. She told Silverlake she'd arrange for Latham to be his advocate, but her main desire is to protect the Royal House from any blowback. I think she feels guilty that two of the children she sponsored ended up in Grimsley's hands."

Simon didn't say anything about the near incineration of Silverlake, nor about Liam's intervention and obvious attraction to Rebeka.

"Siri and Jochim?" Hal asked.

Simon leaned forward and tapped the files on his desk. "The other two kids were Gerling and Astrida Harmish. I'll get Kermal on that tomorrow. They were Ox clan and may have been from the East End."

Hal stroked his beard. "Stillwater is selling kids West? I never figured him for a slaver."

"Slavery's illegal, even in the Havens," Simon pointed out.

"Tell that to the Orcs who end up tenant cropping on some Elf *Syr's* estate," said Hal.

"I thought you wanted Orcs to stay in their proper place," said Simon.

"Proper, yes," growled Hal. "Not licking some Elf Lord's boots."

Simon laughed. "We'll make a Free Thinker of you yet, Hal."

Hal grunted. "So, I suppose you already know that Horace Silverlake runs the linen supply company and that he's your prisoner's cousin."

"Yes," said Simon. "Did he have a sledge in the capitol the night the bodies were dropped at Lily's?"

"He can't say." Hal crossed the room and sat on the couch. "Not officially. But he had six out on deliveries overnight, three of them on circuits that usually take several days. He doesn't track mileage on the sledges, so he doesn't know where the drivers went, only that they were all back in the stables on time."

"Right." Simon grew thoughtful. "So we can confirm a connection between the Silverlake cousins, and we have a witness placing one of Horace's sledges in the capitol at the time the bodies were dropped there. We can connect the dead children to Hiramis by his own words and by the smocks they wore. We shouldn't have much trouble getting a warrant to search the company sledges for trace. It would help if we could narrow it to a specific sledge."

"I have the registry numbers for the three that were out on longer trips," said Hal. "We can start there. Not likely a driver would risk a trip all the way to the capitol if he had to be back in West Faring by daylight."

"Get them to me in the morning and I'll go to the Justice. You and Jack can serve Horace as soon as you can make the drive to West Faring."

"What about the other Silverlake?" asked Hal.

"We've got him on child endangerment and if any of the kids wasn't an orphan, accessory to kidnap, maybe to murder. He's not going anywhere, even with George Latham on his side."

"I'm thinking it may not be a bad thing if Latham gets him bonded out," said Hal thoughtfully.

"I suspect he's lying about being able to contact this Grimsley," agreed Simon. "But I don't see how that helps us much. Grimsley won't be returning to the Cloister now that his game has been blown."

"Aye, you're right about that." Hal took a pipe out of his pocket and spent some time packing and lighting it. "But Stillwater still has a pick in that ground. You can bet that he'll want to keep the shipments going. I'm thinking he'll lean on Hiramis to reach out to Grimsley and set up a meeting. If nothing else it gets the Silverlake cousins out of the middle. They'll lose money but I don't think they want to carry the weight now that we're on to them."

Simon frowned. "I can see that, but how do we benefit? We've got no way to find Grimsley or the Elf he says he works for. And as far as I know, we don't have anyone inside the 'Lollies who can tip us off when Stillwater gets in touch with Grimsley."

"Snick can help us there," said Hal. "He's not a Loblolly, but he has a big family. Remember the cousin who tipped him to that farmhouse bomb factory?"

Simon tamped down the anger that rose up as he recalled the turkey trap the Azeri's had set in the house that had nearly killed them all.

"It so happens," Hal continued, as he blew a cloud of smoke at the ceiling. "that said cousin used to run with one of Stillwater's enforcers. Married to his sister, in fact. Snick can find out when the meet will happen."

"So we set up nearby, get eyes on Grimsley and track him back to wherever he comes from," said Simon.

"Unless you really have a problem letting Silverlake out of the cells."

Simon thought for half a second. "He won't go far. He's too attached to his school." *The Princess won't be happy, but Liam can convince her that Silverlake will get his due when the KP takes the case to trial.*

"Then let's hope Latham is as good as everyone says he is."

Simon rubbed his eyes, fatigue suddenly catching up with him. The fragrant smoke from Hal's pipe was making him sleepy and his eyes felt like they were full of sand. "I doubt anything will happen before tomorrow or the next day. I'm going home. Muster at seventh hour tomorrow as usual. With luck, I'll get the warrant by ninth and you and Jack can serve it. Check with Kyle Evarts about assigning a forensics team to go with you. Any chance Horace will bolt, or put up a fight?"

"Nay," grunted Hal, tamping his pipe but not puffing more smoke. "He's got a solid alibi for the time frame and thinks he's in the clear. He can claim he knows nothing about anything his driver might have done after the sledge left the yard."

"Right then. My love to Molly. See you in the morning."

"I'll do that, lad." Hal stood and tapped the pipe out into a battered tray near the arm of the couch. "And she'll be expecting you for dinner at Week's End. She'll want a full report on your holiday with Sylvie."

"Since when did my love life become a topic of dinner conversation?"

"Ever since you passed your thirtieth Name Day without a wife," said Hal. "She may have raised three other sons, but you'll always be her baby."

Simon sighed. The overbearing Dwarven mother, playing matchmaker for her children may have been a comedic stereotype, but like many stereotypes, there was an element of truth in it. "I'll be there, but what goes on between Sylvie and me is our business."

Hall just laughed. "Try telling that to your foster mother this Week's End." He clapped Simon on the shoulder and left the office, still chuckling.

Simon checked the messages on his desk mirror before giving the incantation to shut it down. He was just crossing the squad room, waving to several of the night shift Keepers he knew, when the summoning tone of his hand-held mirror sounded.

He was surprised to see the ancient face of Elvira Cairns, the Dwarvish secretary to Captain Axhart, in the mirror. It was well after twenty-first hour and she should have gone home long ago. "Mistress Cairns. What can I do for you?"

"You can report to Captain Axhart as soon as possible so that I can go home to my supper," she said in a weary tone.

"I'm on my way."

She canceled the spell without another word. Simon continued across the squad room and drew some curious looks from the night shift when he started up the ancient stone staircase toward the command level rather than heading down toward the stables.

His mind raced through the events of the past couple of days. He'd sent a preliminary report on the dead children up to Axhart's office but doubted that the Captain would want an urgent update this early in the investigation. He briefly wondered if Harold had said something to Axhart about the Princess and Liam but quickly dismissed it. Harold wouldn't want to risk exposing Rebeka as a latent mage by making an official complaint about Liam. Had that weasel Killian complained about Simon's taking over the case? Or about his handling of Nose Kronska's request?

Now that's a possibility, he admitted to himself *But why would Frank tip his hand like that? Better to let the meeting go down. If it went sideways he could always blame me, and if it keeps the peace between Stillwater and Kronska, he can claim credit.*

Gelbard Axhart, current commander of the Cymbeline District Peacekeepers was an exception for a Dwarf. He had risen to command through the ranks, but unlike Hal, whom Simon knew had refused promotion half a dozen times, Axhart actively sought advancement. Most Dwarven Peacekeepers preferred to remain on the streets, or in the background. Simon supposed it was something in their nature that made them shun higher rank and the responsibility that came with it. Certainly Hal could have had Simon's job three times over, but had accepted his foster son as his Sergeant rather than take "that load of horse shit called responsibility" onto his own back. Loyalty to family, team, and the King, in that order was the calculus by which Hal lived his life. That and plenty of good Dwarfish ale.

Simon knock twice on the door to Axhart's office, then

pushed it open. Elvira Cairns was just lifting an oversized flowered carpetbag from her desk in the office anteroom. She favored him with an annoyed glare.

"Go on in." She hooked a thumb toward the inner door. "They're waiting for you."

"They?"

Mistress Cairns bustled past him into the hallway. "Make sure the door locks when you leave," she said without looking back.

Simon pushed open the door to the inner office. It was a large room with dark hardwood paneling and high bookshelves on two walls. A gleaming walnut desk faced the door across a wide floor covered in green and gold patterned Glenharrow wool carpets. Two low-slung sofas covered in green leather faced each other between the door and the desk. Axhart stood facing the door, leaning comfortably against his desk in shirtsleeves, breeches, and hose, his uniform jacket slung over the back of the polished wooden desk chair that he favored.

Simon drew himself up to salute his Captain but Axhart waved a hand at him.

"Stand easy, Sergeant." Axhart'sdeep baritone held only the faintest of Dwarfish burr. "This is an informal meeting."

Simon relaxed slightly and stood at ease, only then looking to the two other occupants of the room. His heart fluttered when he saw Sylvie Graystorm seated comfortably on the right hand sofa. It took all of his self-control to keep from breaking out in a broad grin. Sylvie acknowledged their connection with a slight shake of her platinum blond head and an amused sparkle in her green eyes.

On the left hand sofa sat a tall Elf in the severe charcoal colored dress uniform of the Special Enforcement Division, the Gray Rangers. Olive skinned and black haired, he had the sharp features and violet eyes of the Free People. His rank insignia identified him as a Senior Ranger. This could be none other than Rulanis Summerfield, Head of the

SED's Law Enforcement arm. The Elf regarded him coolly as Axhart made introductions.

"Sergeant Simon Buckley, this is Senior Ranger Summerfield. Ranger Graystorm I believe you already know." Simon thought he saw a hint of a smile on Axhart's lips as he mentioned Sylvie.

Simon bowed to Summerfield then reached out to shake the Elf's proffered hand. "Good meeting, Ranger Summerfield."

The tall Elf gripped his hand. "Good meeting, Sergeant. I recall your name from the Flandyrs affair. Unfortunately, we haven't caught him yet."

"I'm sure you will eventually, sir. I doubt he'll return to the Commonwealth in any event." Simon turned to Sylvie, struggling to remain professional as he shook her hand. "Good meeting, Sylvie."

She for her part remained cool and businesslike, but gave him a sly wink when her boss looked away toward Axhart.

"So Gelbard," said Summerfield. "How shall we proceed?"

"Sergeant Buckley and Ranger Graystorm worked well together in the past," said Axhart. "I'd say we pair them up again and assign Sergeant Buckley's team to the case. Like as not, it connects with their current investigation. Sergeant Buckley will be in overall command for anything here in the Commonwealth, and turn it over to Ranger Graystorm if the team needs to follow leads into the Havens."

"Acceptable," said Summerfield. "Will the Crown sanction a Gray Ranger on a Peacekeeper team?"

"Oh, aye," said Axhart. "They've done it before and the Justice Minister will do whatever I bloody well recommend or she'll find herself another Peacekeeper Commander. D'ye think you can sell it to the Steward if my team needs to cross the Border?"

Summerfield said, "Leave that to me."

"All good then."

"Begging your pardon, sir," said Simon. "But what are we talking about here?"

Axhart and Summerfield exchanged a look. "Rulanis?" said Axhart.

Summerfield nodded. "Two weeks past, one of our Borderlands patrols came across three Orcish children wandering in the fens south of the Anvil River. At first the patrol thought they had come from a nearby estate but the *Syr* there denied them. The children spoke no Qetchwa, and little enough Common Speech. Fortunately, one of the Rangers recognized the language they spoke amongst themselves as a dialect of Southron Azeri. Once they found a translator, the story became even stranger.

"The children had come from Cymbeline, at least as best the translator could gather. An area of the capitol known as East End. They knew their address and their parents were contacted. The parents are Azeri refugees, undocumented. They claimed they had apprenticed the children to an Overseer who promised to place them in a school in the Northwest Territories of the Commonwealth. And get them Commonwealth citizenship." Summerfield frowned.

"The children were picked up by the Overseer near their home and spent several days locked in the back of a travel coach with a number of other Orc children. From their description, it sounds like they crossed the border somewhere near Portalis and ended up in a large empty building out in the countryside. Rather than a school, the place looked like the slaughter pens they had known from home. I am told the East End of Cymbeline is the center of the meat packing industry. They saw the wooden pens spread across the floor and became frightened. They were able to slip through a gap in the rear doors and ran."

Sylvie took up the story at a sign from her boss. "From their story, we were able to narrow down the area of the building they were in. It was an old flax barn just south of Portalis near the main highway to Talien. It was empty when our team raided the place, but there were a dozen livestock holding pens inside, just as the children had described. From the sanitary pots placed in the pens and from aural analysis, it was clear that at least sixty Orcs had been in those pens within the past two days."

"All children?" asked Simon.

"Can't tell from the trace left behind, but it corroborates the lost children's story," Sylvie replied. "We spoke again to the *Syr* from the nearest estate. At first he denied any knowledge of the barn but when we brought up the subject of his own worker's immigration status, he became much more talkative. The barn was the site of regular auctions of Orc children and young teens, sold to bidders from estates all over the Havens. Technically, not slaves. They all had signed contracts of indenture from parents or guardians in the Commonwealth. Seven years indenture to the contract holder and then they were free to go. By which time they would be so deeply in debt to the estate that they would be bound for the rest of their lives paying it off."

Simon knew the swindle well. Indentured workers were charged outrageous prices for their food, for rent on their meager dwellings, for clothing and 'equipment'. And although they were paid a fair wage during their indenture, it was not near enough to cover the charges. They ended up hopelessly in debt and virtually enslaved to the estate. The Commonwealth had ended the practice a century ago, but it was still business as usual in the Havens. "So how does this connect to our current case?" he asked.

"When we questioned the indentured workers on the *Syr's* own estate, a name came up. Whispered, no specific information, but a name: Biran Stillwater. The Orcs wouldn't confirm that he was behind the smuggling of children, but they connected him to it."

"Any connection to our dead children?" Simon asked.

Sylvie frowned. "Just rumors. Some of the younger Orcs told of children being used for evil spells at some other estate. Never a specific place or a specific person. But they all talk about 'young ones from the East.'"

Simon's face was grim as he added, "All of the dead children were likely under the age of ten. Siri Marshstrider had just had her Name Day ceremony." To Axhart's inquiring look, Simon added, "We have names now on all of the dead children, two pairs of siblings, all Azeri Ox clan. I'm sending Kermal Brackenville to the East End tomorrow to find the parents of Gering and Astrida Harmish. "

"All good," said Axhart with a wave of his hand. "Send me regular reports on your progress. I'll leave it to you and Ranger Graystorm to work out the details of sharing your information. Any thing else, Rulanis?"

The Senior Ranger shook his head. Both Simon and Sylvie took that as a dismissal. They saluted and left the office together. In the outer office Sylvie smiled and looped her arm through Simon's.

"So, does the team still muster at seventh in your office?" she asked.

"Aye." Simon's pulse quickened. "I'm thinking it would save time and resources if we went over the evidence tonight at my flat and drove in together in the morning. In the interest of efficiency, of course."

"Of course." Sylvie laughed. "But I've booked a suite at the Royal on King's Road. It's bigger and far more comfortable than that closet you call a flat. And they have Room Service."

CHAPTER TWELVE

If anyone at Wycliffe House noticed that Simon and Sylvie arrived together in Simon's sled the next morning, no one mentioned it. Nor did anyone take note of the rumpled state of Simon's uniform, as if it had been left on the floor overnight and hastily donned less than an hour earlier.

Hal did give them a knowing smile when he entered Simon's office just before seventh and found the two of them sipping coffee and going over the forensics reports on the dead children.

He greeted Sylvie warmly with a bear hug and gruff, "Good to see you, lass." Molly had granted Sylvie 'Rights of the Hall' in House Stonebender several months earlier, making her practically family, and Hal had taken a proprietary attitude toward her ever since.

Jack and Liam entered shortly afterward, followed closely by Kermal. Sylvie greeted Jack with a firm handshake, Liam with a brief embrace, and then looked expectantly at

Simon.

Simon swallowed a gulp of coffee. "Oh, sorry. Sylvie Graystorm, meet Kermal Brackenville, the team's armorer. Sylvie is on loan to us from the Gray Rangers."

"Good meeting, Agent Brackenville." Sylvie stepped forward and extended her hand, as Jack and Hal found seats on the couch.

Kermal took her hand and bowed over it. "Good meeting, Lady Graystorm."

Sylvie laughed. "I'm the youngest daughter and no Lady. Please just call me Sylvie."

Kermal straightened and his face colored. "As you say, Sylvie." He turned to Simon. "I thought about it overnight, Sarge. If you need me to use my family connections, I will; but you should understand how dangerous that might be."

Simon ignored the puzzled looks from the rest of the team. "Hopefully it won't come to that. We've gotten some new information since yesterday afternoon."

Sylvie perched on the arm of the couch next to Hal. Kermal remained standing, not quite at attention. Simon quickly went over the interview with Princess Rebeka and Hiramis Silverlake, glancing at Liam who shook his head slightly. Simon did not mention Rebeka's ability as a new mage. "So, Silverlake is in custody, at least for now. George Latham has been endorsed as his advocate, so he may get a bond. We're actually hoping he does and that he makes contact with Sailesh Grimsley. The Orc is our only link between Silverlake and Stillwater. We believe it was Grimsley who transported the children west and into the Havens." He turned to Sylvie. "This is where our investigation and yours connect. Tell the rest of the team what your people have found on your side of the border."

Sylvie told them about the lost Orc children, the barn with its holding pens, the auctions and the indenture contracts. As she spoke, Kermal's face darkened and his mouth drew down in a deepening frown.

"The indentured Orcs wouldn't speak openly about the sales, although clearly they knew about them. I daresay some of the children in their own quarters came from just such purchases. What they did give us was a name: Stillwater."

"Biran Stillwater," said Simon. "Chieftain of the Knacker Street Loblollies. He's an Azeri, Wolf clan, but he had deep ties to Snake Clan and Hargash Barsaka's Azeri Liberation Brigade before we put them out of business."

"So there is a reason for Ox clan to think they're being targeted," said Kermal.

"How's that?" asked Hal.

Kermal reddened as Sylvie turned to look at him "There's always been friction between Ox and Wolf. And Serpent, or Snake, Clan fancies itself the leader in what they call 'the struggle for liberation.' Most Azeri's in the Commonwealth, especially the undocumented ones, couldn't care less about overthrowing the Empire. To them it's just exchanging one master for another. They only want to be left alone."

"So why Ox Clan?" Liam asked.

"Ox has been in the Commonwealth longer than most," answered Kermal. "They were the knackers and tanners and meat cutters in the Empire, low class work. Always on the bottom of the Clan hierarchy. When they started coming here a hundred years ago, they were treated as tradesmen. They could even own a business. The last thing Ox Clan wants is a return to the old ways. Wolf and Snake have always been top Clans in the Empire. They figure they should be here, too. Stillwater's big in the Wolf Clan, has the ear of the Chieftain if the rumors are right. The Clan leadership can't officially sanction him, but he's probably got half of the Clan Council on the payroll. If he's selling fake indentures, Ox is were he'd go for product."

"They're children," muttered Hal.

Kermal faced him, his lip curled in disgust. "Aye, they are. Orc children. But to Stillwater, they're nothing but a commodity."

"Peace, lad." Hal held up his hands. "I'm with you on this dig."

"Kermal," Simon said into the brief uncomfortable silence that followed. "I'd like you to go back to the East End today. Talk to the parents of Gering and Astrida Harmish. Find out if they were legally apprenticed or if they simply went missing. I'm sorry to stick you with the job, but you'll likely be the one telling them the kids are dead. Do you want me to assign a Grief Advocate to go with you?"

"No, Sarge," Kermal shook his head. "It's a Clan matter. I'll speak to the local Matriarch first. She'll know who to send with me."

Simon touched Kermal's shoulder. "Sorry, shitty duty. You know what's best for your own people."

"What about the warrant, lad," asked Hal.

"I sent the request to Justice Longwood with the first courier this morning. He's the duty Justice for expedited warrants today. Should have an answer before ninth."

Hal got to his feet. "Jack, you're with me. We'll draw a sled and put a forensics team on alert. Anything else?"

"That's it, for now," said Simon, and the two Dwarves stomped out together.

"Liam, I want you out at Caledonia University. Talk to anyone you know in Fire magic. See if they can shed some more light on this Blood spell Gran Swampwater mentioned."

"I'll ask around," Liam said. "But doubt anyone will know much. Blood magic of any type is seriously frowned on over there."

"Any other ideas?" asked Simon.

Liam considered his question for a second. "There's always the Library. I'll likely need a warrant to access the Restricted Collection, though."

"Maybe a *Demilvosk* shaman?" suggested Kermal hesitantly. "My father was a *demilia,* don't you see."

"Hex magic?" Simon asked. "Do people really believe in that?"

"Well, they do use a lot of Blood magic in their animal sacrifices," said Liam. "Might be worth a shot."

"Do you know any *demilia* who would be willing to talk to us, Kermal?" Simon asked.

"No," the Half-Orc said. "Not really. I'm a Pathist myself. There's a *Demilvosk* shop just south of Lily's tavern on Canal. It sells the fetishes and herbs they use in the rites. But I don't know the shopkeeper, only the shop."

"All good," Simon said. "Sylvie and I will check there first. Maybe Lily has a contact as well."

Kermal and Liam took their leave and headed toward the stables.

Sylvie settled on the arm of the couch, facing Simon. "Do we really need to know that much about the actual spell?" she asked. Simon had told her about the meeting with Gran Swampwater and the rumors of children being used for some sort of life draining Blood spell. "I mean, Blood magic of that type is illegal on both sides of the border. Someone cast a Blood spell, at least with those four children. We know Grimsley took them into the Havens. Like as not, they were bought at the flax barn auction just before our teams raided the place. We find Grimsley, he leads us to whomever bought the children and we arrest that person."

Simon forced his gaze away from Sylvie's long legs. "Without specific knowledge of the spell, we won't be able to check the caster for any forensic evidence. Unless the caster confesses to the crime, we'll have no real case. We can charge them with the purchase of illegally indentured Orcs, but they could claim they purchased what they believed to be legal contracts. The children may have just run away, like the kids you found wandering in the fens."

"But someone transported the bodies back to the Commonwealth," Sylvie pointed out. "That implies remorse and a desire to return the children home. Anyone who'd use them for a Blood sacrifice wouldn't want them found again."

"Do you think it likely that Grimsley did that," Simon asked.

Sylvie pursed her lips "No. I don't, but someone did. Maybe someone connected to the spell caster."

"I agree," said Simon. "But even identifying who bought the kids is a long way from having enough for an arrest. And Grimsley's still in the wind."

The warrant came in by office messenger five minutes before ninth. Simon signed it and had the messenger run it down to the stable where Hal and Jack were waiting. He and Sylvie followed and Simon drew a nondescript unmarked sled to look for the *Demilvosk* shop that Kermal had mentioned.

They found the place three blocks south of Lily's in a narrow alley off of Canal Street. Simon looked up at a goat skull, complete with curled horns, hanging above a worn ironwood door. The skull was smeared with a red pigment, paint Simon supposed, as it was too red to be blood. The door had once been red as well, with heavy cold iron bolts spaced across the top and bottom. The paint had faded to a dull maroon and rust stains streaked the wood below the bolts. There was no number on the door, no sign announcing the shop's purpose, only that goat skull. Simon and Sylvie stood before the door and exchanged glances.

"I guess they don't get much casual custom," Sylvie observed.

Simon pushed the door open. A small bell attached to the doorjamb tinkled as they entered.

"We don't serve tourists or gawkers." A bored sounding high-pitched voice called from the darkened rear of the shop. "And we don't do interviews with journalists or grad students."

Candles and a weak glowglobe cast more shadows than

light through the interior of the shop. A long counter ran down the left side of a single open room. Behind it, drawers and shelves held bottles of colored liquid, bundles of dried herbs, goat and cow horns, strips of animal hides, and an array of colored candles of various lengths and thickness. Tables covered with wolf hides, ox tails, snakeskins, dried fish, bundles of camel hair and the skulls of ten or twenty different animals filled most of the floor space. On the back wall, hung a tall tapestry lit by six-foot candelabras and an altar nearly encased in the wax of a hundred different colored tapers. The air smelled of spice and dried grass, overlaid with a faint hint of blood and rotting flesh. Something moved in the deep shadows next to the altar and Sylvie's hand flew to the hilt of her rapier.

"Stay your hand, Elf," said the same voice. "We don't tolerate violence in hallowed places." An ancient appearing Orc stepped into the faint light of the candles. He was almost man height but skeletally thin, draped in a red silk robe and a cape of black fur. He held an ironwood staff topped with the skull of a wolf and entwined with colored ribbons and dried grapevines.

Sylvie placed her right hand on her chest and bowed. "Forgive me, *demilia.* You startled me."

Simon asked, "Are you the proprietor of this shop?"

The Orc's eyes narrowed. "I am the *demilia* of this place. I have various religious items that are available to the faithful. My name is Forsaka, Rivers in the Common tongue. How may I assist the King's Peacekeepers today." His words were polite but his tone said something else.

"Mr. Forsaka." Simon acknowledged him with a bow. "I'm Sergeant Simon Buckley, Magic Enforcement squad. This is Ranger Sylvie Graystorm, SED from the Borderlands. We'd like some information about Blood spells."

"Blood," scoffed Forsaka. "Always the Blood. *Demilvosk* worship uses the Blood sacrifice of animals to connect with the spirit guides sent by the Gods. We don't cast Blood curses or sacrifice babies to the full moon or practice witchcraft. Those are ancient lies. If you really want to know about Blood magic, ask the Witches down South. They make a regular practice of it."

"Peace, *demilia,*" said Sylvie. "We only seek information."

"We have spoken to the Mother of the Spirit House," added Simon. "She wasn't able to help us. She said a member of my team, an Orc, might have more information. He's the one who suggested we seek out a *demilia.*"

"An Orc Peacekeeper?" Forsaka asked. "What name and family?"

Simon recalled the formula Kermal had used in introducing himself to Marshal Greenmire. "Kermal Brackenville, son of Hasfal, born for Wind Clan by Sheila, daughter of George Willows."

Forsaka's eyes widened, but otherwise his face remained impassive. "You'd better come with me." He turned and walked to the tapestry in the rear of the shop. Pulling it aside, he led them into a small but brightly lit room with a desk, a small cot and a table surrounded by four chairs. A commercial salamander sat on a rolling cart next to a small sink and faucet near the back corner.

"Please, sit." Forsaka leaned his staff against the wall. "Tea?"

Sylvie started to refuse, but Simon held up a hand . "Tea would be welcome." To Sylvie he whispered, "Food or drink, offered and accepted. Ritual."

They took chairs next to each other, facing the door. Forsaka noticed, but only smiled.

"The fact that you're here together suggests that both the Magic Squad and the Rangers have a case involving Blood magic. Are you merely lovers, or are you working together officially."

"Our relationship is none of your concern," bristled Sylvie.

"Perhaps not." The Orc set a kettle on the salamander

and activated the heating spell. "Or perhaps it is. How old are you. Lady Graystorm?"

"That also is none of your concern." Sylvie's voice was now cold in a way that Simon had heard before when anger had pushed her to the edge of her self control. She seemed to draw inward, become more aloof and regal, suddenly every inch the High Elf that she was.

The Orc cocked his head, regarding her. "No longer a youth, but still young enough to be rebellious. Over eighty, certainly, but not more than one hundred fifty. One twenty, give or take a year?"

Sylvie remained silent, rigid with anger.

"What does that have to do with anything?" asked Simon.

"You're here because four Orc children were found dead, killed in a Blood magic ritual," said Forsaka as he dropped tea into the kettle and set it on a metal tray. He turned to face them. "A Ranger and a Peacekeeper working together means a connection to the Gray Havens. And you don't see how your relationship is part of this?"

Sylvie came out of her chair in one fluid motion, drawing her rapier and holding the tip to Forsaka's throat. "Explain yourself, Orc. How do you know about the children, and how do you know about the two of us?"

Despite the rapier at his throat, Forsaka chuckled. "All of the Hollows knows about the children. As to the two of you, I could see it in your eyes and the set of your bodies as soon as you entered. Now put away that silly blade and sit down. Then we'll talk like civilized people."

Sylvie stood unmoving until Simon spoke quietly to her. "Put the sword away, Sylvie. We need his help."

Sylvie slid the rapier home in its scabbard and sat stiffly, muscles still tensed. Simon noted that she subtly shifted away from both him and the Orc. Simon tried to catch her eye, but she looked straight ahead. Forsaka set the tray on the table, seated himself, and poured three cups of fragrant tea as if nothing had happened. Simon took his cup and sipped. The tea was chamomile, flavored with cardamom.

"Why do you think our relationship has anything to do with these children?" Simon set down his cup.

"Surely the Witch in the South told you about the Blood spell," Forsaka said. "And still you can't figure it out?"

"She didn't know any specifics," said Simon. "She just talked about *ghiras* and *strahk* and transferring life from one person to another."

Forsaka looked expectantly at Simon.

"But what spell? How does it work? Gran Swampwater implied that the spell drained the life of the caster as well."

Forsaka waved dismissively. "What of it, if the life is long? So long that years or even decades wouldn't matter."

Sylvie stiffened. "You're saying an Elf did this evil? Killed these children? No. No Elf would be part of such a thing."

"But a filthy Orc would, right m'Lady?" Forsaka said bitterly. "Who else would be willing to cast such a spell? Who else would have the need?"

"Wait." Simon told Sylvie as she started to rise from her chair. "Just wait. If an Elf did use those children in a Blood ritual, what would he or she gain?" He looked back to Forsaka who held his eye for a moment and then looked at Sylvie. "Unless it could be used to prolong the life of another person."

Forsaka gazed into his tea. "You begin to see, Human. The truth of your own circumstance is the key. Who would risk so much, and why? Only a person obsessed with the life of another."

Sylvie sat silent, not looking at either Simon or Forsaka. The Orc turned his face toward her. "Why are you here, m'Lady, if not to find this truth? The children were taken to the Havens alive and returned here dead. To find the person who sacrificed them, you must find someone whose need was great, bonded to one who is willing to commit any act to meet that need."

Simon stared at Sylvie. *Did she not see the implications of what Forsaka had said, or did she just not wish to acknowledge it?* If the children were sacrificed to perform some kind of life enhancement or life prolonging spell, who would be the most likely target? A Human bonded to an Elf, either a spouse or lover or someone of great importance. The irony of his own situation hit him and her anger and disbelief seemed less cold and more personal. He couldn't ignore that all leads they had followed so far pointed to the Borderlands, not to the Northwest. It made sense, but Simon knew that was a long way from proof, or even real evidence.

"How do you know so much about this Blood spell?" Sylvie's tone was glacier cold. "What are you not saying? Is it because you cast it yourself as part of some secret Orcish rite?"

"If I had cast such a spell, we would not be speaking now. We Orcs are very good at avoiding Bluebelly questions when we need to." Forsaka gave her a sly smile. "No, m'Lady. Like it or not, this abomination comes out of the Gray Havens. That's where you'll find your answers."

Simon touched Sylvie's arm. She didn't look at him, but at least she didn't pull away.

"What do you know about an Overseer by the name of Grimsley?" asked Simon.

"Sailesh?" Forsaka sneered. "He's a toad. Serpent Clan, no Family. Fancies himself a gang captain, but hasn't the steel for it. Why?"

"We have information that he has been transporting these children West, at least as far as the border, maybe beyond. Dealing in false indentures and selling the children at auction in the Borderlands."

"Ha! Moving in with the big wolves is he? Who is pulling his strings? Grimsley hasn't the brains or the nerve to have thought of that himself."

"We believe he's working for Biran Stillwater, or at least

working with him," said Simon.

Forsaka grew thoughtful. "That makes more sense. Stillwater has few friends down here in the Hollows. He and his Loblolly boys have abandoned their own kind. They all act as if they have no Family."

"We can't link Stillwater to the dead children, but we can make a case against Grimsley," said Simon. "Do you have any idea where we can find him?"

Forsaka pulled at his lower lip and looked speculative. "If I had such information, Sergeant, it would be difficult for me to reveal it to you."

"Why would you protect scum like Grimsley," asked Sylvie, her voice still icy.

Forsaka looked her in the eye, defiant. "Not him, but one who might have shared a confidence with me. In my role as a *demilia*."

"Priest's seal?" Sylvie's tone was scornful. "I wasn't aware that such a thing existed in *Demilvosk*."

"Not formally," said Forsaka. "Nothing like the seal of a Temple Virgin, or a Priest of the Blessed Mother. But I depend on the trust of my people, and they expect me to maintain their confidences."

"What can you tell us?" asked Simon.

"That Grimsley is not in Cymbeline. That he favors a certain tavern in Portalis where Orc laborers congregate. A tavern owned by an Orc in Grimsley's debt. Beyond that, I am bound to say nothing."

Forsaka drained the last of his tea and set the cup upside down on the table—food offered, accepted and finished—signaling that this meeting was ended.

"Thank you, *demilia*." Simon drained his own cup and set it next to Forsaka's. "You have been very helpful."

Sylvie left her unfinished tea on the table and rose to her feet. She gave Forsaka a brief bow, cold and distant, then turned and walked out.

By the time Simon reached the sled, Sylvie was already

seated on the passenger side, her sheathed rapier across her knees. She traced the filigree hear the hilt with her fingertip, but said nothing as Simon climbed in.

He muttered the incantation to activate the Air spell, then made a U-turn on Canal and headed north toward Wycliffe House.

As they passed Lily's, an elegant, dark-colored sled passed them heading west across the Knacker Street bridge. It caught Simon's eye because it looked out of place down here in the Hollows where most sleds were worn out junkers or ostentatiously tricked out gangsterslides. But his mind was occupied, focused on Sylvie's rigid posture, her angry reaction to Forsaka and his own unease at the Demilia's remarks.

They rode in silence up Canal for a ways, the traffic getting heavier as they approached the city center. Two blocks from Tanner Street, Simon had to pull to the side to let a Fire Brigade sledge roar past, its alarms blaring and its orange and green warning lights flashing.

Sylvie turned to him as he pulled back into traffic. "I will be one hundred twenty four on my next Name Day."

Simon glanced at her. "Yes, all good."

"Simon, I'm ninety years older than you are."

He kept his eyes on the road ahead. "Yes, I can add and subtract."

"Stop being dense, Simon," Sylvie said angrily. "To most Humans I look thirty and will for neigh on to forever if I don't get killed on the job."

"So it should bother me that I'm falling in love with an old lady?"

"Simon!" Her tone was exasperated, but now she actually smiled.

Simon smiled back. "I don't care, Sylvie..I care about you. I love our time together. I want more of it. Does it bother you? Is that why you get distant after we're together for a day or two? Do I seem childish to you?"

Her face fell. "Oh, Gods, Simon, no. It's just that I don't know what to do." Her eyes filled with tears that spilled down her cheeks. "I love you and I don't want to watch you die."

"Is that all? Hal's told me a dozen times if I don't watch out, I'll get myself killed before I make Lieutenant. You may not have to wait very long."

"Be serious."

Simon slowed the sled and pulled it to the curb. He turned in his seat to face her and took her hands in his. "I am serious," he said. "I can't imagine living without you, Sylvie. But I know it's a possibility. It's something we both know and have to face if we're going to be with each other. I wanted to die when I lost Alira, but I didn't. I can't bear thinking about losing you, so I don't. I know I can survive it, but I won't waste time worrying about it." He raised her hands to his lips and kissed her fingers. "Is that why you pull away from me when we've been together for a few days? You're thinking about me dying someday?"

She squeezed his hands. "How can I not? I know the day will come, even if the job doesn't get you first. No matter what happens, I will outlive you, and that's a fact that I can't forget."

"Why not? Look, Sylvie, I don't know what kind of future we can have together; I just know I want to share it with you. I don't care how old you are, I love you."

She pulled her hands from his and gazed out at the passing traffic on the street. "I know, Simon. And that makes it harder."

"It doesn't have to be." His voice sounded plaintive, even to his own ears.

She said nothing.

After a lengthy silence, he restarted the sled and pulled away from the curb.

As Simon guided the sled into the stables beneath Wycliffe House, it occurred to him that the elegant sled he'd seen on Knacker Street had been dark green with gold trim. *Was it a Royal livery? Was Rebeka in the Hollows visiting Lily?*

CHAPTER THIRTEEN

They climbed the stairs to the squad room in uncomfortable silence. Simon felt helpless. He knew he'd somehow failed to tell Sylvie what she'd needed to hear when she'd revealed her true age, but what the hells did she expect? He'd long suspected she was far older than she looked, and he truly did not care. All he wanted was to be with her and feel the same commitment from her. The future, he'd learned, never turned out quite the way one wanted it to, so why worry about it?

Liam was waiting for them in Simon's small office. He cocked his head at Simon, picking up on the strain between him and Sylvie, but Simon shook his head slightly and Liam leaned back on the couch.

"Anything to report from the University?" Simon asked with forced casualness.

"Nothing particularly useful," said Liam. "Like I said, no one over there wants to talk about Blood magic. I put in a request in your name for a warrant to get into the Restricted Collection, but it likely will take a day or two before it gets approved."

Simon smiled at Liam's willingness to assume he would back him on the request for the warrant. So different from the tentative, almost shy, young Fire mage who had reported to the team only a few months ago.

"Good, it's still worth pursuing, although we may have a lead on the caster's motive." Simon filled him in on their conversation with Forsaka. "All of our information points to the Borderlands." Sylvie pressed her lips together, but said nothing. Simon continued. "I think our next move should be to try to find this tavern in Portalis that Forsaka mentioned. If we can't get a lead on Grimsley here in the Commonwealth, maybe we can find him there."

Sylvie sank onto the couch next to Liam.. "You're right. I still find it hard to credit an Elf with Blood magic, but then, I wouldn't have believed there was a market for kidnapped children in the Havens either. I'll talk to the Rangers at the Borderlands station. There can't be too many Orc owned taverns in Portalis."

Simon looked at her and this time she met his eye..

"Are we all good?"

She smiled but still seemed troubled. "I just need a little time to call the Havens. Muster at seventh tomorrow?"

Simon took her question as a sign that he'd be staying at his own flat that night. Not as he'd have liked things, but he wouldn't press her.

Sylvie stood and said good night to Liam, touched Simon on the back of the hand and left the room.

"Everything all good, Sarge?" asked Liam.

"All good." Simon glanced at the timepiece on the wall. "You might as well go home too, Liam. It's too late in the day to get much done. I'll wait here for Hal and Jack." As Liam stood to leave, Simon asked, "Are you going to see Rebeka any time soon?"

"I'm meeting her at the Palace after eighteenth tonight. Why?"

"See if she was down at Lily's this afternoon. Don't push or make her think it's important. Just see if she was there."

"Why, Simon?"

Simon drummed his fingers on his desk. "I thought I saw a sled with Royal livery colors heading up Knacker as we were leaving the *Demilvosk* shop. Just wondered if it was the Princess."

"I'll check into it." Liam left Simon alone in the office.

Simon checked his messages but there was nothing important. He glanced at the timepiece, again. It was just before sixteenth hour. Too early to go home but too late to get much done. He might as well write up his notes from the interview with Forsaka.

He had just started when there was a knock on the door to his tiny office.

An office messenger entered and handed him a gray envelope. "This just came from the public liaison desk for you, Sergeant Buckley. The duty Agent said an Orc dropped it off and said it was urgent. We cast a Reveal on it. Doesn't show any signs of toxins or spellcraft."

Simon thanked him and slit open the envelope. It contained a single sheet of paper folded and sealed with wax. Embedded in the seal was a lock of coarse black hair. The note written on the paper was short.

Tonight. Twenty-second hour, Lily's tavern. You and three other Keepers. Farsk Kronska.

Simon sat back in his chair and rubbed his chin. He'd almost forgotten about the meeting between Kronska and Stillwater. He briefly considered mobilizing the rest of the team to take Stillwater into custody. They had little more than hearsay linking Stillwater to the auctions in the Havens. Hiramis Silverlake might be willing (or be induced) to testify that Stillwater had sent children to the school, and that those children had been picked up and transported away by Grimsley. But they had nothing directly linking Stillwater to the auctions, or to specific children. Simon was reasonably certain that Stillwater would have covered himself well.

He considered calling Kermal to see if the Harmish children had been legally apprenticed or simply disappeared, but thought better of it. He doubted the parents would testify in any event, and there was this meeting between Stillwater and Kronska to consider. Simon had pledged his word and reputation that the parties would be safe on neutral ground. If he showed up with an arrest team and didn't have a solid case against Stillwater, it would look like he and Nose had set the whole thing up. It would spark a gang war rather than avoid one.

Nothing we can do right now except go through with the meeting. He sighed. He'd better call Killian before it got any later.

Killian answered the summons to his mirror right away. "Yes."

"I just heard from Kronska," said Simon. "The meeting is on for tonight, Lily's place, twenty-second hour. Two of your guys, you and me. Will you want to meet there, or ride together from here?"

Killian frowned. "I have to get in touch with my guys. They're in the field, so likely better to meet somewhere nearby and arrive together. Coming all the way back to the House seems a waste of time."

"Agreed," said Simon. "Corner of Canal and Tailor Alley at half past twenty-first? There's a public stable there. It won't look suspicious for several sleds to pull in at the same time."

"Sounds good. I still don't like this."

"I know, Frank. I'm the one with his neck out. If something goes sideways, you're covered."

Killian didn't say anything, just broke the connection with a wave of his hand.

Simon looked at his notes again, then pushed them aside. They would wait. He wanted something to eat and a change of clothes before going back into the Hollows. He summoned Hal's handheld as he pulled on his jacket and shut down his desktop mirror.

"Evening, lad." Hal's face shimmered into view as the connection opened. "Jack and I are still out in the wilds of West Faring. Like as not be here all night. Evarts' team is still going over the laundry sledge."

"Any joy?" asked Simon. Right now, any hint of a break would be welcome and give him something to think about besides Sylvie.

"Well, we've definitely got the right sledge now. The mages found traces of Orc hair and a couple of drops of blood in the cargo bed. We've got a line on the driver, too. Orc by the name of Fenreed. Resident of Portalis, of all places. Drives the route through the Borderlands for Silverlake's linen company."

"Have you questioned him?"

"Not yet. Didn't come to work today. We've got an address, but we'll need you and Sylvie to come out here if we're going into the Havens."

"Sylvie and most of the team have gone for the day," said Simon. "We got some more information on the Blood spell, and a lead on Grimsley that points to Portalis as well." He didn't mention the question of Sylvie's age and how it might relate to the case. "But that's on hold for now. Nose Kronska reached out. The meeting with Stillwater is on for tonight."

"Who's backing you up?" asked Hal. "I don't like the idea of you going in there without me."

"Killian and two of his guys from the Civil squad," said Simon.

Hal scoffed..

"The deal was me alone with Killian and two men, Hal. Nose and the Scalpers know your face. Even if you tried to stay in the background, someone would make you for a Keeper. This is touchy enough without Stillwater getting the idea we're there to get him."

"I know. Doesn't mean I like it, though."

"Not much you could do from the House that would be any different than where you are now. I promise I'll be careful."

Hal's eyes narrowed. "See that you do. Molly will have my hide if something happens to you while I'm out of town."

"Good night, Hal" Simon broke the connection. He decided to go home before heading into the Hollows for the night.

By half past twenty he was in the Oxley, heading south on Canal. He'd showered and managed to sleep for two hours before getting up at twentieth and dressing in dark blue breeches, matching hose and loose fitting white shirt. His jacket hung low enough to cover the needler in a belt clip holster at the small of his back. The Reaper he wore openly in a scabbard on his left hip.

As he crossed Tanner just east of Wycliffe House, his mirror chimed. He swiped a hand over its surface and Lily Ponsaka's face appeared.

"Mistress Ponsaka," he said cautiously. "What can I do for you?"

"You have a man here in my tavern who needs looking after," she said. "I know you and Killian are on your way here. Nose Kronska has set himself up on the south wall with some muscle and your Agent is already making them twitchy."

"What man? And how do you know about the meeting with Kronska?"

"What kind of innkeeper would I be if I didn't know what was going on in my own place?" Lily sneered. "Besides, this peace talk with Stillwater is good all around. I have sources in both camps, don't you know."

"Which man, Lily?" Simon repeated.

127

"Brackenville, that Wind Clan half-breed you have on your team. He's been in here since just before eighteenth, drinking hard and clearly not an Orc who's good at it."

"Drunk?"

"Cork high and bottle deep. You need to get him out of here before he causes a scene and gets in the way of this parlay."

"I'm on my way." Simon pushed the sled faster. "See if Hack can get him over to the bar. At least he'll be away from the tables."

"Aye," said Lily. "Best you hurry, though."

Simon sent Killian a quick message that there had been a change of plans and he'd meet him at Lily's. He sped down Canal faster than was legal or prudent but didn't run into any Civil patrol sleds on the way. He turned west on Knacker and parked the Oxley on the street next to the lot where this whole business had started a scant three days earlier. He immediately noticed the green and gold Simpson Coachworks sled parked across the street from him. It was unmarked and the windows of the passenger compartment were blacked out, but the man in the driver's seat wore a chauffeur's uniform with a martial air. There was nothing overtly obvious about the sled or the driver, but Simon was sure he was either military or Palace Security. Which meant the Princess was here.

Gods damn it, can things get any worse? Simon thought. He almost crossed the street to confront the "chauffeur" but thought better of it. If Harold had trained him, Simon would get nothing from him other than silence, or maybe a needle in his face if he got too aggressive. Instead he turned and made for the front door to the tavern.

He paused in the tavern door. The tension in the air struck him first. Conversations continued, either in whispers or loud bluster, but it was clear that attention was focused on the south corner of the room, farthest from the door. Kermal sat at the end of one of the long tables that ran down the center of the room, a bottle in front of him and a glass in his hand. He faced the back corner where Nose Kronska sat alone in a round booth, his back to the wall. Kronska looked relaxed, but the three bodyguards arrayed in front of him looked alert. Simon was surprised to see they were Human, not Orcs.

The men were high-priced security operatives—fit, unsmiling and businesslike. The kind of men who did their job and did it well, whether the job in question was running a security spell at the door to a nightclub, guarding a lowlife gangster, or shooting you dead. All would be done with the same dispassionate efficiency. At the moment, the focus of their professionalism was Kermal Brackenville.

Simon surveyed the room. Something was wrong. He marked four other Scalpers seated at tables facing the door. *Was Kronska expecting trouble? Or looking to start it?*

He crossed the room and stood next to Kermal. He made a small palms-down gesture to the nearest security man, hoping to reassure him that the situation was under control. Kermal picked up the bottle and poured another glass of brandy.

Kermal looked up at him. "Sit down, Sergeant," he slurred at Simon, not taking his eyes off of Kronska. "Have a drink with me."

"You need to pull yourself together, Agent. You can't stay here."

"Why not?" Kermal lifted his glass and took a long swallow. "Something important going down?"

"You are close to an insubordination charge," said Simon. "Now get up and go home."

"Not on duty, not in uniform, so not under your orders." Kermal took another swallow. "Home? You know what home is to the Harmish family? A packing crate. A gods damned packing crate for two adults and three kids under the age of five. I did what you said. Told them about their son and daughter. They didn't cry or carry on, just nodded and thanked me. Told me they would have had to turn them out on their own soon anyway, so's the little ones would have enough to eat. It was like a gift from Matra when that Overseer offered to place the older ones in a school for Orcs."

Kermal drained his glass. He reached for the bottle, but Simon put a hand on it.

Kermal looked at him."Don't". He pulled the bottle away and poured. "Funny thing about Orc gods. They're all two-faced. Durlash is the storm god, bringer of thunder and lightning. But he's also the judge of the dead. Kitlak is the god of war, but he's the peacemaker, too. And Matra, she's the goddess of the hearth and motherhood; but her other face is the goddess of mourning and sorrow. Which face do you think she showed when those kids were led away by that bastard Stillwater?"

"You're drunk, Kermal." Simon leaned down and said in a low urgent voice. "You're putting this whole meeting at risk."

Kermal glanced at him then looked back at the three men standing in a loose semicircle in front of Kronska's table. "I know he's on his way here. Stillwater. I mean to ask that son of a gnome why. What makes an Orc betray his own kind that way?"

"Not now." Simon leaned closer. "Not here. We'll make a case against him and against the rest of the network. But we can't afford a gang war on top of that. And I can't let you make it look like this was a setup. Now do you get up and follow me to the kitchen so I can get you out of here? Or do I put a sleeper needle in you right now?"

Kermal stared at him, a hard glint in his eye that caused Simon to pull back slightly. Then the Half-Orc blinked and smiled wryly. He drained the last of the glass. "No need for that, Simon. I'll go quietly."

Simon straightened up and looked toward the kitchen. Lily stood there, framed in the large doorway. Behind her

taken out. Whoever that Fire mage was, Kronska knew what was going to happen."

As soon as Simon said it, he knew it to be true. Kronska had not looked shocked or surprised, only satisfied. *Rebeka couldn't have had anything to do with this. There's no way she would even speak to the likes of Kronska, much less plot murder with him.*

Simon shooed Lily back to the kitchen. He checked around the common room more carefully. Another Civil Patrol squad had arrived and locked down the exit, not letting anyone enter or leave. It was a good thing Liam had gotten Rebeka out so quickly.

The room wasn't crowded, but there were still twenty or so people now huddled together at the center table. They were mostly Orcs, with a few scattered Humans, and a lone Dwarf passed out on the floor and snoring loudly. *How do you find a Fire mage in a crowd?*

CHAPTER FOURTEEN

Killian started organizing his squad to begin interviewing the people in the common room. Simon turned back to Kermal and Kronska.

"Give me that weapon, Kermal," said Simon, "And stand down. You've been drinking."

Kermal shrugged, still holding the bolt pistol on Kronska. "Didn't do too badly, for a drunk." He jerked his chin in the direction of dead guards.

"That wasn't a request." Simon's voice hardened. "That's an order, Agent Brackenville."

Kermal's forearm bunched as he gripped the pistol tighter. Then the Half-Orc sighed and relaxed. "Aye, Sarge." He reversed his grip on the bolt pistol and handed it to Simon, butt first.

"Go back to the House, Kermal. Write up a report I can show Captain Axhart. Killian will take this over now and make a big show of it. Best you not hang around here while he does; but you and I need to have a conversation. My office, half-hour before muster tomorrow. Clear?"

"Aye, Sarge,"

Kronska started forward as Kermal headed toward the kitchen doors. Simon raised the bolt pistol. "Sit down, Nose. We need to talk."

"About what, Sergeant? I was just having a friendly drink with my associates. I ain't done nothing."

"Horseshit. You knew what was going to happen here. That's why you brought outside muscle with you."

Kronska held his hands out from his sides, showing his palms. "I ain't armed. I had to make sure I was safe. A man never knows who to trust these days."

"I'm too tired to put up with your crap, Nose," Simon growled. "You set me up. Sit down before I forget myself and put a bolt through your head for lying to me."

"What, you gonna shoot me?" Kronska sneered. "In front of your buddy Killian? You're a Bluebelly and I got rights."

Simon raised the pistol and pointed it at Kronska's head. He took a step forward. Kronska paled and lifted his hands in front of his face.

"Farsk Kronska, you are placed under lawful detention to answer for the crime of accessory to murder. You are under caution that any statements you make may be recorded and used in evidence against you. You have the right to legal counsel before making any further statements to me or to any other King's Officer. Now back up, sit down, and put your hands on the table. Or do you want to resist detention and give me an excuse to shoot you?"

Kronska sat and Simon snapped a set of manacles onto his outstretched wrists. "Not hardly sporting, that," Kronska grumbled.

"Shut up, Nose."

Simon lowered the pistol and rubbed a hand across his face. He knew Kronska had set them up, but there was precious little other than his presence in the tavern to link him to Stillwater's death. He'd not touched a weapon and the only witnesses to prove he'd hired outside help were dead. The rest of his Scalpers would be nothing more than soldiers, following orders to be in the tavern at a certain time and to react when the Loblollies started shooting.

Liam approached from the kitchen, out of breath and agitated. He looked around at the Civil Patrol teams working their way through the crowd, taking names and separating individuals to interview. "Rebeka's on her way home," he said softly. "I got her out before the rest of Killian's teams showed up. I passed Kermal on the way back in. He didn't look good. What's going on, Sarge?"

"What's going on?" Simon's voice crackled with anger. "Why don't you tell me? What the hells were you thinking, bringing her here? She's a Latent, she barely has control of her magic, and now we're looking at a spontaneous combustion death. Gods above and below, Liam. Why not just run up an orange flag if you want to attract attention to her?"

Liam paled. "Hand to the gods, Simon. Rebeka and I had nothing to do with that. The spell was cast outside, at least several minutes earlier. I didn't feel the casting and that blue glow above Stillwater means it was set to trigger when the conditions were right."

Liam was right. Simon hadn't felt the casting either, only the trigger. Maybe the spell was set up for a specific time, or perhaps it was triggered when Stillwater entered the tavern.

"That's not what I mean, Liam," he said. "This was a setup from the first. What was Rebeka doing here?"

"She heard about the meeting from Lily. She was going to confront Stillwater about the kids he was selling West. I told her it wasn't a good idea. I tried to talk her out of it." Liam shrugged. "She's a Princess. She's used to getting her way. I could either tie her up to keep her at the Palace, or come with her and try to keep her out of trouble."

"Did anyone see her?"

Liam shook his head. "Nobody but Lily and the kitchen staff. And they're used to seeing her here. As far as they know, she was just visiting like usual."

Simon glanced toward the door to see Killian striding toward them. "Do you think you can find out who cast the Fire spell, and from where?"

"Maybe," Liam shrugged.

"See what you can find." Liam nodded and started for the front door. He brushed past Killian without a word.

Simon spoke to Killian before he could protest. "Kronska's under detention, Frank, and he's been cautioned. Have your guys found the Fire mage yet?"

"No. Where's Brackenville? And what's Aster doing here?"

"I sent Kermal back to the House. He wasn't fit for duty and wasn't directly involved in this," answered Simon. "I called Liam in to try to locate the mage who burned Stillwater."

"Damn you, Buckley," Killian growled. "That wasn't your call. This is a Civil case and your pet Orc was at least a witness. I saw him holding that bolt pistol when we came in here, so don't hand me that 'not involved' crap. How do I know he wasn't part of this whole set up?"

"Because he took the same oath you did, Frank." Simon's calm voice belied his anger at the insinuation. "And he's under my command. He's not going anywhere but Wycliffe House. You'll get your chance at him. Besides, this is on me. I brokered the meeting and I was the ranking Agent here when it went sideways. You've got a gripe? Take it up with me or take it to Axhart."

"You're damned right I've got a gripe. I told you we were being set up from the start." Killian pointed to Kronska. "He played you like a lute, set Stillwater up to be burned, and now my squads tell me there are bodies spread over half the Hollows. His boys have taken out every Loblolly jolt dealer between here and the Old Wall." Killian drew his needler and stepped toward Kronska. "Who helped you with this?"

"With what, Bluebelly?" Kronska raised his hands, palms out.. "I was all set to have a sit down with poor Biran. Work out our differences, don't you know. Then there was a fire and a bunch of shooting. I hid under the table. Didn't see nothing."

Killian raised the needler. Simon touched his arm.

"He's under detention, Frank. And he's been cautioned. You can take him to the House and question him all you want. Not here."

Killian tightened his grip on the needler, and for a moment, Simon thought he was going to pull the trigger. Then he let out a growl of frustration and lowered the weapon.

"Steelhelm," he shouted back over his shoulder to one of his patrolmen. "Get over here and take this maggot spawn into custody. Get him back to the House and into Booking. I'll be along later to decide what charge to file."

He turned back to Simon. "All good?" he asked as Steelhelm pulled Kronska to his feet and started him toward the door. "Or do you two want to hold hands in the patrol sled?"

"No, but I have some questions for him." Simon kept his voice level, despite wanting to shut Killian's mouth with his fist.

"You can wait your turn back at the House," said Killian. "This isn't your beat and right now you're a material witness yourself."

"Do you want to book me and caution me, too, Frank?" Simon asked angrily. "Or is my word good enough for you?"

"Don't try to play the Temple Virgin with me, Buckley. You're not innocent in this. You and Kronska have a history, I checked it out. What did he tell you to get you to vet this meeting?"

Simon crossed his arms. "You're mining false ore, Frank. Nose wanted to clear the water you muddied by putting it out that the Loblollies had butchered those children as some sort of gang reprisal."

"And you know they didn't? Kronska was looking to start a war for the jolt territory. If stirring up trouble over those kids didn't lure Stillwater into the open, then this meeting of yours sure as hells did." Killian swept an arm toward the rest of the room. "They were set up and waiting. This wasn't a truce talk. It was an ambush."

"I know. I was here. You weren't."

Killian reddened and poked his finger at Simon. "We'd agreed to meet and come together. Why were you here early? What did you and Kronska talk about?"

"What? Nothing. Lily called me and told me that Kermal was here and half drunk. I didn't want him messing things up or giving Stillwater the idea that we had a team waiting for him here."

"How did Brackenville know about the meeting?" Killian demanded. "Was he working with Kronska, too?"

"No! That's just horseshit, Frank. Kermal has his own problems. Yes, he'd been in Loblolly territory today. But he was telling the parents of those kids that their children were dead. It was hard duty. He came here, *off duty*, to get drunk. Who wouldn't?"

"And in his 'half-drunk' stupor he was still able to get the drop on three professionals?"

"I did that," Simon lied. The last thing he wanted right now was to have Killian looking into Kermal's family ties. At least not until Simon had some answers to his own questions about the Half-Orc armorer.

"Right," scoffed Killian.

"Don't believe it, then." Simon shrugged off Killian's attitude. "They were shooting at the door. I was behind the middle one. I hit him with the hilt of my saber, took his weapon, and shot the other two before they knew what hit them. But the one on the left over there managed to get off a shot as he went down. It missed me but hit the guy I'd cold-cocked."

He could tell Killian didn't believe a word he'd just said, but he didn't care. He held out his wrists. "Go ahead, Frank. Slap on the irons if you can't take the word of a fellow Keeper."

Killian glared at him. "Am I going to hear the same thing from them?" He jerked his thumb over his shoulder at the other witnesses that his team was beginning to interview.

"Not my problem. I made my statement. I'll gladly write it up for you and make it official."

"Get the hells out of here, Buckley," Killian snarled. "Captain Axhart is going to hear about this. You can't pull this shit on my beat and get away with it."

Simon reversed his grip on the bolt pistol and handed it to Killian who took it with a puzzled expression.

"Evidence," Simon said as he stalked toward the door.

Outside he took a deep breath of cold air. The smells of the Hollows, damp cobblestones, the lingering tang of curing leather, rotting garbage and woodsmoke, all competing with the ever present wet mud smell of the river and canals, took him back ten years to his beat patrol days. How had he been so blind to Kronska's real plans? Back in the day, he'd have been more suspicious, would have done some checking on his own, before agreeing to the meeting. Nose was now firmly in charge of the jolt trade, and the other gangs and big players in the Hollows would believe that the Peacekeepers, or at least Simon, had helped him. Not only that, but his main suspect and only real lead on the dead Orc children was gone. Killian would go straight to Axhart and Simon would be lucky to get off with only a suspension.

Liam cleared his throat, and Simon jumped. He hadn't heard the mage approach.

"I found out a couple of things, Sarge. Over here in the alley." Liam led Simon a few steps to the left where a narrow passageway, barely wide enough for the two of them to stand side by side, ran between Lily's building and the one next door. An old Orc, down on his luck and far beyond his best days by the look of him, waited for them there.

"This is Vike," said Liam. "He lives here."

Simon wasn't sure if Liam meant the Hollows, or this alley in particular, but from the wizened old Orc's looks, he supposed the latter.

"He has some information for us, but first, I wanted to show you this." He pointed to a spot at his feet. Simon bent down. Faint runes had been chalked on the rough pavement. Wan light from the street filtered in at an angle, and as Simon shifted his head to get a better look he caught the faint glint of gold in one of the lines. He bent closer. A thin thread of gold, not much wider that a hair was fused to the paving stones.

"The spell was cast from here," said Liam. "Probably just as Stillwater got out of whatever sled brought him to the meeting."

"So it was triggered when Stillwater crossed the threshold to Lily's place," said Simon. "What about friend Vike, here? Did he see it?"

"Aye, Boss, that I did." Vike's voice held the coarse rasp of an old leather tanner. "I got me a little nest about five yard back that way. I saw an Orc dressed in a fancy red cloak marking the ground with a piece of chalk. Then he takes out a pouch and sprinkles something on the chalk marks. Then he has words with that new Bluebelly chief what's been busting heads around here the past six weeks. The Bluebelly crosses the street and waits while a big black sled pulls up. The fancy Orc waves his arms about for a second and then this little blue flame flies out of his hand and jumps to a big Orc what's getting out of the sled with a bunch of Loblolly hard boys. I thought the big Orc would catch fire then and there, but he don't. He just shakes his arm like it was cold or something and then goes over to Lily's door. I don't want no trouble with an Orc what can do magic, so I slipped back to my nest."

"Where is the Orc that cast the spell?" asked Simon.

The old Orc shrugged. "Don't know, don't care."

"You're sure it was Patrol Agent Killian who spoke to the Orc mage?" Simon asked.

"Din't ask his name," Vike said. "But he knocked me about last week for begging a few coppers down on the quay. 'Twas the new Boss Bluebelly on the Hollows beat, and that ain't no dross."

Liam and Simon exchanged a look. The Orc noticed.

"I ain't in no trouble, am I?" Vike asked. "You promised me half a crown if I talked to your Boss."

Simon dug a crown out of his pocket and handed the coin to Vike. "No trouble. Just don't say anything to anyone else. Especially not to any of Killian's men."

Vike took the coin eagerly and faded into the darkness at the back of the alley.

"The gold was to augment the Fire spell." Liam pointed at the markings. "He'd have had to make a more complicated casting for it to be delayed like that. Two level probability cascade at least."

Simon's knowledge of quantum magic was rudimentary, but he did understand that gold augmented Fire spells and that casting an immolation spell with a delayed trigger was complex business requiring the skills of a Master. *Can't be too many Orc mages with that level of skill. There's a lead to follow, if I can still trust Kermal.*

"And Vike seems pretty clear that Killian spoke to this mage well before Stillwater's sled pulled up." Simon rubbed his chin. "Which means Frank and his team were already here when the ambush went down. Why were they hanging back?"

"Do you think Killian knew what was going on?" Liam

asked.

"Seems so. I can't think of any other reason for him to be waiting outside, or to be talking to an Orc mage."

"But why?" asked Liam. "Was he maybe waiting for you to show up, not knowing you were already inside? And maybe he was just checking the mage out, you know, shaking him down for loitering or something?"

Simon considered it, but shook his head. "No, I sent Frank a message that I'd be waiting at Lily's. We were supposed to meet ahead of time, but Lily called and warned me that Kermal was liable to make a scene. And if Frank was shaking the mage down, why did he let him stay in the alley. He'd have moved him on or detained him rather than jeopardize the meeting. Unless he knew it was an ambush all along."

Liam stared at him. "Look, Sarge, I don't like the man either, but why would he be party to this? It'll start a gang war on his turf and there's never been any love between Killian and Kronska."

"Lesser of two evils?" suggested Simon. "It's no secret that Killian was pitting the gangs against each other. He as much as told Hal and me that he'd be happy to see them kill each other off. Maybe he thinks he can control Nose, or can manipulate him if he owes a favor."

"Big risk, that," said Liam doubtfully. "Suppose Kronska decides to weasel on him?"

"Frank must have something on Nose that's just as dangerous," said Simon. "Cave in's make for strange allies."

Liam still looked doubtful. "Want me to cast a Reveal on this stuff and see if I can identify the mage?"

"You can try," said Simon. "But likely he's skilled enough to mask his aura."

"Want me to get the Civil patrol guys out here?"

"No. I want to keep this close until I can see what Killian's going to do. Go on home, Liam. Muster at seventh in the morning."

Aye, Sarge." Liam looked uncomfortable, but walked off toward the corner. Simon assumed he had a sled or flyer parked nearby. He bent down and touched the chalked runes on the pavement, but felt nothing. He remembered another Orc mage who had been tremendously powerful.

Joby Blackpool had fooled him with a folksy country Orc persona, when in fact he'd been a Master, the most skilled mage Simon had ever encountered. But Blackpool was dead and Simon knew of no other Orcs with similar skills. It occurred to him that despite his years in the Hollows and his close association with Lily, and even Kronska, he knew little and understood less about Orc society than he'd imagined. Kermal's fighting skills, the presence of an Orc Fire mage of exceptional power, even Forsaka's knowledge of the dead children, had all taken him by surprise. And surprises left him feeling very uneasy.

CHAPTER FIFTEEN

Simon arrived at Wycliffe House a few minutes after sixth hour to find the place buzzing with activity. Civil squad sleds were lined up in front of the Central Booking doors, each with a full load of Orcs in their rear detention compartments. Simon recognized several Peacekeepers, but they were all too busy to engage in conversation. Most either didn't notice him, or ignored him.

He made his way up to the squad room, where the pace of activity was even more hectic. Most of the desks were occupied and all of the interrogation rooms were in use. He managed to catch the eye of Servi Lillihammer as she arrived for the day shift. "What's going on, Servi?"

"Gang war." Her face grew hard. "After your little affair last night, all hells broke loose on the streets. The Loblollies are getting the worst of it. Most of the higher ups and almost all of their street level jolt dealers are dead or in hospital. Some of their enforcers managed to get their shit in a stocking and hit back, but Kronska and his closest boyos are in hiding. What the hells were you thinking, putting Nose and Stillwater in a room together?"

"Why isn't Kronska in custody?" demanded Simon. "I put him under detention myself and turned him over to the Civil squad."

"Take it up with Frank Killian. Half an hour after Kronska was booked, some fancy Kings Road advocate showed up and demanded a bond. Killian could have fought it, but no one could reach him. The night Magistrate had no choice. Still, the bond was high; 5000 Crowns is what I heard. And Nose paid it without blinking an eye."

"Of course he did. That's less than half a days take from the jolt trade." Simon wasn't surprised that Killian hadn't been available. His outrage in Lily's bar had been an act. He clearly had some stake in Kronska's play for the jolt trade. Without an Agent to testify, the King's Prosecutor, likely a low level new hire, wouldn't have had any grounds to contest the bond. But where was Nose getting the high-powered backing to hire professional bodyguards and expensive advocates?

"He hasn't got the trade locked up yet, if the fighting down in the Hollows is any measure." Lillihammer waved at the barely controlled chaos around them. "I've got to go, Simon. You'd best be keeping to the shadows for a few days. Can't imagine the Ax is going to be very happy about all this."

Simon watched as Lillihammer walk to her desk calling out to her Sergeant to give her an update. He crossed the busy squad room to his tiny office and sat down behind his own desk. Servi was right. If Killian hadn't filed a formal complaint with Captain Axhart yet, it was only a matter of time before he did. If Simon hoped to keep his badge, he'd have to find the link he was sure existed between Killian and Kronska.

He mulled over what he knew. Kronska had set him up,

that was clear. He'd planned the meeting as an ambush. Somehow, Killian knew about it and held back until the immolation spell had triggered and the Loblollies were down. *Did he know for sure, or was he waiting for me, like he claimed? Am I being suspicious because I don't like the man?* No, Vike said Killian talked to the mage in the alley. He knew what was going to happen. But Killian had gone out of his way to make trouble for the Scalpers. He'd gotten a reputation in the Hollows for violence and harassment. How could Nose trust him? How could Killian trust Nose? And why hadn't Killian objected to the bond?

Simon looked up as he sensed someone in front of the desk. Kermal Brackenville stood at attention, his eyes fixed on a point above Simon's head. His winter blues were freshly cleaned and pressed and his scalp freshly shaved. He looked pale and tired, but he was holding himself rigidly erect.

"Agent Brackenville reporting as ordered, Sergeant Buckley," Kermal said, his voice a bit too loud.

Simon glanced at the timepiece on the wall. Thirty minutes before seventh hour, to the second. "Oh for the gods' sake, Kermal, stand at ease. How are you feeling? All good?"

Kermal eased into a more relaxed position. He still didn't meet Simons eye. "Well enough. You wished to speak to me?"

"Don't shut me out, Kermal," said Simon quietly. "I don't know where you learned to move like that, but you may have saved lives last night, maybe even mine. I don't want to play the hardass here. Just talk to me."

Kermal went rigid for a second, then relaxed. "*Kul ghiras annan sarngal.*" His shoulders sagged. "Spirit follows the Blood. I'm my father's son."

"But you said he'd left the Cabal's service."

"I said I didn't know what he really did." Kermal rubbed his clean-shaven scalp. "But even that wasn't strictly true.

He trained me. Starting from the time I could walk, he taught me how to move, how to fight, how to look at a scene and assess it for threats or opportunities. I didn't know what he was training me for. I thought, when I got a little older, that he was just preparing me for the world. Life can be tough for a Half-breed. He was trying to make me able to stand up for myself. Or so I thought."

"When did you find out the truth?" Simon asked.

"Not until he died, just after my sixteenth Name Day." Kermal sighed and eased down onto the arm of the couch across from Simon. "Actually, I think I knew by the time I was ten. Tenth Name Day is important to Orcs. It's when you receive your True Name, the one your parents speak for the first time in front of the Clan; the one you will carry with you out into the world. There were men at the ceremony that I didn't know. They weren't family or friends. Some were from different clans. When I asked my mother about them, she just said they were friends of my father and that I shouldn't mention it again. But I could see that she was afraid of these men. That most of the Clan was afraid of them. They left right after the ceremony, but I remembered their faces. I remembered the one who was at my father's death rites, six years later. That's when I knew for certain who my father really was."

"And you've had no contact with them since?"

Kermal hesitated. "Not directly."

"What does that mean?"

Kermal stood at rigid attention. "It means I don't speak to them or work for them. I'm a Peacekeeper. I'd be bound to report any criminal activity."

"But?" Simon urged.

Kermal's stance eased a bit. "But I think they send money to my mother. She left the city after my father died. She lives out East, near the Gorges. I send her money from my salary, but she keeps insisting she doesn't need it. I found out a couple of months ago that she's been depositing everything I send her into an account at Great Eastern bank, here in the capitol. A joint account with both our names on it."

"Can you document the money you send her?"

Kermal stiffened. "Do I need to?"

"Not to me." Simon folded his hands and looked down at the desktop "But you're in a high profile unit now. Never give even the appearance of being on someone's cuff. The Inspector General can make the most innocent exchange look shady. And after last night we may all be under the IG's gaze."

"All the money I send her is a regular distribution from my pay. The clerks will have the paperwork."

"All good then," said Simon. "I don't need to tell you to keep your background inside the team. Right now, you and I, and maybe Liam, are the only ones who know."

Kermal looked away. "I don't like keeping secrets, Simon."

"Neither do I, and I hate asking you to keep this one. But I may be under the sword soon over this Stillwater business. Better for you and the rest of the team if the Cabal and your father's real job stay out of the mix."

Kermal nodded. "Any thing else?"

"No, but stand easy for a few minutes. Liam and Sylvie will be here soon. Jack and Hal are still out by the Borderlands. We'll mirror them once we get organized for the day."

Liam arrived a few minutes later, looking more haggard than Kermal. He slumped onto the couch.

"Rough night?" Simon asked.

Liam glanced at Kermal. "A certain young woman summoned me about an hour after I left you," he said. "She was distraught and needed to talk. I ended up going to her and didn't get home until after fourth hour."

"How did you get past Palace Security?" Kermal laughed at Liam's stunned look,. "Come on, Liam. Did you think you could keep a secret down in the Hollows?"

"Lily?" asked Liam.

Kermal's lips quirked up in a smile. "She's proud of the Princess, like she was her own daughter. And she thinks 'that half-Elf conjurer' might be the right person to help her find her way. I'm not sure what she means by that, but it's obvious the two of you are involved somehow."

"Well, keep it close, will you? Her father doesn't know. As to security, she's the Princess. She gets what she wants." Liam looked at Simon. "Harold asked me to remind you of a conversation the two of you had?"

"He's suspicious of your intentions."

"Oh wonderful," groaned Liam. "I'm a dead man."

"What's this about dead men?" asked Sylvie as she glided into the office. She wore her Ranger uniform with the breeches and high boots, her rapier slung at her left hip.

Simon smiled in spite of himself. Just the sight of her cheered him. "Romantic entanglements." He gave her a wink.

"Ah, yes," said Sylvie, looking Simon in the eye. "Those can be complicated, can't they?"

Simon gazed back at her. Her look seemed both playful and full of promise. He wondered if it were just wishful thinking on his part or if she was trying to close the rift that seemed to have developed between them.

Kermal coughed discretely, and Simon blinked and shook his head. "Brace up, Liam. We may have a busy day ahead depending on how last night's troubles play out."

"What troubles?" Sylvie settled onto her usual perch on the arm of the couch. "Do they have anything to do with the hornet's nest out there in the squad room?"

"Aye. And our mutual case may be side tunneled for a while." Simon quickly filled Sylvie in on the ambush at Lily's and the subsequent fighting between the Loblollies and the Scalpers. "The nugget of it is that our best lead on finding Grimsley and the rest of the network that's been selling

back me."

"Then why worry?"

"Because in the mean time, Grimsley will know Stillwater is dead. He'll go to ground, or he'll talk to whoever bought those kids and they'll have time to cover themselves. We may lose our only chance to solve this case. I need to find Nose and make him talk. He didn't have the money or the brains to plan that ambush. Someone is backing him."

She stood and came around the desk and put a hand on his shoulder. "Then we'll find out who." She leaned in and touched his cheek. He turned his head toward her and they kissed. Not long or passionately, but full of feeling and promise.

"Does this mean we're all good?" he asked as she pulled her mouth away from his.

"We always were." She smiled.. "I just needed a little time to figure it out."

"I meant what I said about ..." he stopped as she touched his lips with her forefinger.

"I know."

He wanted to kiss her again, but the summoning tone of his mirror interrupted. Sylvie smiled again and stepped back as he dug it out and swiped it on.

"Mistress Cairn," he said when he saw the Dwarfish woman's face. "What can I do for you?"

"Captain Axhart wants to see you as soon as possible," she said.

"Now?"

"His actual words were, 'right gods' damned now'."

"Aye, I'm on my way." He waved off.

"Should I come with you?" asked Sylvie.

"No, I don't think the Ax wants to see you."

"So what can I do?"

Simon thought for a moment. "Get us clearance to go into the Borderlands, to Portalis and to that auction barn. Hal and Jack have a lead on the driver of the laundry sledge, an Orc from Portalis. Even if we don't have Grimsley, the driver may give us a lead on wherever those children were killed."

"I talked to Summerfield last night. We should have visas and a writ by tomorrow." She touched his cheek with the back of her hand. "Meet back here in an hour?"

"Will do.".

They left the office together. Sylvie went to check on the writ and Simon climbed the stairs to the command level.

Elvira Cairns glanced up as Simon opened the door to Axhart's outer office. She pointed to the inner door and returned to the papers she was shuffling on her desk. Simon knocked at the door.

"Enter," came the reply.

He crossed the green-carpeted floor and came to attention in front of the desk. "Sergeant Buckley reporting, Captain."

Axhart didn't speak for a long minute. He sat watching Simon's face, letting him hold his brace at attention. Finally he glanced down at the papers on his desk and shook his head. "At ease, Sergeant. I just had a conversation with Frank Killian. He's filing a formal complaint with the IG claiming you colluded with an Orc named Farsk Kronska to lure Biran Stillwater into an ambush."

"Captain, it wasn't like that."

"No? Suppose you tell me what it was, then. Because once this gets to the IG, I'll be having to explain to Tintagel why my best Sergeant is on suspension."

Simon ignored Axhart's backhanded complement. "I told Kronska I'd be at the meeting to assure Stillwater the tavern was neutral ground. Kronska told me he wanted to negotiate a truce between the Scalpers and the Loblollies. According to Kronska, Killian had been stirring the pot down in the Hollows, setting the gangs against each other." Simon paused and shook his head. "I'll admit it. Kronska played me. He was planning the ambush all along. But, hand to the gods, Captain, I had no idea that it was anything other than a talk on neutral ground."

"And yet Killian says you knew something was going to happen. You changed the plans, went to the tavern early and had half your team with you rather than going alone." Axhart sounded more curious than angry, which Simon chose to see as a good sign.

"Agents Brackenville and Aster had no knowledge of the meeting," answered Simon. "Kermal had done a difficult death notice that afternoon and was in need of some support. Liam went along to talk to him, not to be part of the meeting. I heard from Lily Ponsaka that Kermal and Liam were there and went to tell them to go home."

"And Stillwater just happened to arrive while the three of you were the only Peacekeepers in the tavern?"

"I know how it looks, Captain," said Simon. "But Frank Killian was there when the immolation spell was cast on Stillwater. He spoke to the mage who cast it. He could have been inside when the attack started. Instead he kept his men waiting across the street until Agent Brackenville and I had subdued Kronska and his Scalpers had taken down the rest of the Loblollies."

"And you can prove this?" Axhart's eyes narrowed.

"I have a witness who saw Killian speak to the mage, but he's a vagrant. The only name I have is Vike. Like as not he's hiding out somewhere in the Hollows. But the spell was cast by a master level mage. Liam found the casting circle and traces of the gold he used to augment it."

Axhart sighed heavily. "I'm inclined to believe you over Killian, but this is official now, or will be as soon as the IG gets wind of it. What I believe won't matter then. You need to get in front of this quickly. I can hold it up for 48 hours or so, no more."

Simon swallowed hard. "Aye, sir. I need to find Nose Kronska. Someone is backing his play for the jolt trade. He hired professional Human bodyguards, ex-military by the look of them and not cheap. Plus the mage who immolated Stillwater has skill. Liam tells me it was at least a two level probability cascade; that's master level casting. Nose doesn't have the resources for that kind of sophistication."

"Then you have a job of digging to do, and fast. As I said, I can give you 48 hours before the roof caves in. Don't waste it." Simon turned to leave, but Axhart stopped him. "I don't like the idea that one of my Agents could be on the cuff to some Orc gangster. There will be no mercy for anyone who is, whether Killian or someone else, am I clear?"

"Aye, sir."

hook on his belt, likely a habitual gesture. "We din't get notification of a Magic Squad operation in th' area. What gives, Buckley?"

Simon made a placating gesture with his left hand as he holstered his needler. "The operation was initially just a routine investigation. Follow up on a crime discovered in the capitol but likely committed in the Havens. We went to interview a witness near the Eastern gate when this idiot did a runner. He's wanted in connection with the deaths of four children and the illegal transport of dozens, possibly hundreds, more. His name is Sailesh Grimsley. Check your watch alerts, he's likely on them as an Apprehend and Hold."

Utzler nodded. "I recollect seein' that on th' squawk yest'day. You needin' a hand?"

"Obliged." Simon smiled. "We're headed to the Portalis crossing in a couple of hours. Can you hold him in your station until I can summon the House and arrange transport back to Cymbeline?"

"Will do. McCandle?" The second Keeper started forward at his Sergeant's call. Between the two of them, they got Grimsley settled in the rear detention compartment of their sled. By that time, a medic unit and a tow sled had arrived to clear the crash scene. Simon gave Utzler a quick report of the chase and was glad to learn that there had been no other injuries or accidents as a result.

"Can you give me a couple of minutes to talk to him before you take him in?" Simon asked. "He's been cautioned."

Utzler glanced at the Orc in the Patrol sled. "Suit yourself. You need me to be busy elsewhere?"

"No, just a couple of simple questions. This case is tangled enough without raising an issue of unnecessary force."

He found Grimsley slumped in the back of the patrol sled. The Orc flinched as Simon opened the door and bent down to Grimsley's eye level. "Where's Horace Silverlake?"

Simon asked.

"How should I know?" The Orc whined. "Ask his cousin. They were always thick, the two of them. Looking down at the likes of me."

"I'll ask one more time," said Simon. "Horace was the go between for you and the school. Stillwater pulled the strings, but kept himself insulated from the hands-on work. Hiramis talked to Horace who passed the orders on to you. Now, I have four dead kids and a trail that leads straight to you and Horace. You're on the hook for those four deaths unless you can point me toward someone else. Stillwater's dead, so you're next in line. Where is Horace Silverlake?"

Grimsley said nothing, staring straight ahead at the back of the seat in front of him.

"So be it." Simon straightened up and waved toward Utzler.

"Wait," said Grimsley. "I didn't have nothing to do with those kids getting dead. I took them West, sure. But the papers was all in order. I just took them to the barn, got paid and went back home. Anything else is on Horace. He knows who runs them indenture sales. He's connected over on the other side."

"Where is he?"

"Gone. Hand to the gods, I don't know nothing else. He did business in my ex-wife's sister's tavern. Over Havenside, in Portalis. She owes me for getting her set up in the place. Makes for a good meet-up spot when we got business there."

"Names?"

"She's called Fenreed. Gretl Fenreed, but I think that's her married name. My ex was a Hansaka girl."

"Husband wouldn't be named Tobit, by chance?" asked Simon.

Grimsley bowed his head. "Wouldn't know. We ain't been that close since my ex left." He looked up at Simon, his eyes filled with fear and pleading. "You'll put in a word hand. Simon did some figuring in his head and relaxed. Jack hadn't been driving too much over the speed limit if he was still west of the Ring road. *Unless he stopped for breakfast.* He decided to leave that rock for another day.

They filled Liam in as Simon drove. They reached the Portalis crossing in a little over two hours. Simon bypassed the busy commercial checkpoint and pulled into the diplomatic lane. They were waved through when Sylvie flashed her Ranger credentials and they crossed into the Borderlands.

"Portalis, or Borderlands Station?" Simon asked Sylvie.

"Borderlands," she said. "They may have information on Silverlake if he's registered as a business agent in the Havens. And based on Liam's suggestion, we can start tracking gold sales in the province. Assuming, that is, that our killer is somewhere in the Borderlands."

"Fair bet," said Hal. "We're certain Silverlake's sledge took the bodies to the capitol. Between the time of death and the time they were found, there isn't any other possibility."

"What about customs and immigration?" Liam leaned forward in the back seat. "Wouldn't his passport have been registered if he entered through the Border checkpoint?"

Simon shook his head. "He's an Elf. Right of return to the Homeland, even though he's of the Free People."

"He may still have been recorded," said Sylvie. "If he declared any imports, for instance, or exchanged Crowns for Elfcoin."

Simon followed the main route toward Portalis for a few miles before turning south on a wide divided highway toward Tallien. They drove through mile after mile of farmland with white fences marking off wide fields of cotton, flax, wheat and indigo. Stately homes in the Elven style dotted the country side, all domes and spires set off with wide lawns and flowering gardens. Eventually Sylvie directed Simon to a side road. They passed through a small forest of oak and elm and came to a low, wide building partially built into a green hillside. There were spaces for sled parking in front and a steep drive led below ground to a sheltered stable area.

Simon drove down into the stable and parked. Sylvie led the way to a secured entrance, flashed her badge and spoke a few words. Simon felt a thrill in his arms as the security spell on the door lifted long enough for the group to enter. They followed Sylvie up a wide stair to a large open room very much like the squad room back at Wycliffe House. Rangers in uniform moved purposefully about, some working at desks, others talking to colleagues.

A tall, dark-haired Elf looked up from a large magic mirror and grinned, showing perfect white teeth. "Sylvie Graystorm," he said. "Well met."

"Well met, Hamil Fairborn." Sylvie extended her hand.

The dark Elf rose and gripped her hand with both of his. "Where have you been?" He eyed Hal, Liam and Simon. "Have you been collecting strays?"

"Hamil Fairborn, meet Haldron Stonebender, Liam Aster, and Sergeant Simon Buckley, King's Peacekeepers all."

Fairborn reached out a hand and Simon shook it. The Elf's grip was firm and somehow questioning. "So, you're Buckley."

"Disappointed?" Simon stiffened.

Fairborn laughed. "No, not at all. You did brave work on the Flandyrs case." He looked at Sylvie. "He suits you."

Sylvie frowned. "Not now, Hamil. We're here on business."

"Fair enough. I've been expecting you. The Boss told us to give you whatever you needed." Fairborn bowed slightly toward Hal and Liam. "The rest of your team, I presume. You'd be Aster, the Fire mage. And Haldron Stonebender is a name known even here in the Havens. Well met."

He extended his hand and Hal shook it.

"Well met, Hamil Faiborn," said Hal, his voice gruff. "What would you be hearing about the likes of me?"

He climbed out of the sled and removed his jacket and lanyard. He unbuckled his sword belt and handed the scabbarded Reaper to Sylvie. He unclipped the belt holster with his needler, tucked the weapon into the waistband of his breeches, and bloused out his shirt to cover it. The early Spring weather was a bit cool to be walking about in shirtsleeves, but Simon doubted anyone in the tavern would notice.

"Wait for my signal," he said.

Sylvie leaned across the driver's seat. "Be careful."

Hal made a sour face but didn't object.

Simon took one last look around before starting across the gritty and rutted street. As he reached the boardwalk in front of the tavern and started to step up, he felt a sharp tingling pain at the base of his spine. He stopped and spun around. Someone nearby was casting a Fire spell. He glimpsed a tall golden-haired Elf with hands outstretched in his direction. He dove to the muddy street, and the world exploded around him.

Heat seared his back followed by a palpable wave of sound and broken glass. Flames erupted from the broken windows and shattered doorway of the tavern. Simon lifted his head from the muddy puddle he'd landed in looking left and right for the Elf, but the man had vanished.

Simon struggled to his feet, slipped in the mud and fell to his knees. Sylvie rushed to his side. Hal made for the tavern door but was driven back by the intense heat. There was no sound other than the roar of the fire; no screams, no shouts, not even the sirens of the fire brigade. Hal raised his arm to protect his face from the intense heat and peered into the flames, then turned away.

Sylvie helped Simon to his feet. "Did you see him?" he asked. "The Elf?"

Sylvie shook her head.

"What Elf?" asked Hal.

"The Fire mage, the one who cast the spell; a little taller

than Sylvie, blonde hair, green jacket, dark green breeches and white hose. He ran that way as soon as the tavern blew." Simon pointed up the alley where the mage had disappeared.

A few people, Orcs and one or two Humans stood across the street from the tavern. Simon stretched a kink out of his back and stared at the blazing building. Somewhere behind him he heard the wail of the Fire Brigade siren. Even from the opposite side of the street, the heat was intense enough to be uncomfortable. The flames had already consumed the first two floors and were licking at the roof.

"Get back, lad." Hal tugged at his sleeve. "There's nothing you can do for anyone inside. They're already gone to the Green Lands, may the Mother give them rest."

Simon started to turned away. Then he stopped. "Hal, do you have a home address for Tobit Fenreed?"

"Aye," said Hal, pulling a notebook from his pocket. "Wrote it down here somewhere."

"Sylvie," said Simon. "Get in the sled!" He grabbed Hals arm. "We need to go, right now. I'll drive, you find that address."

"What's the rush?" asked Sylvie. "Shouldn't we wait for the Fire Brigade?"

"No time," said Simon. "If Tobit's still alive, we need to get him under wraps before that Elf can burn him, too."

A few minutes later, Simon stopped the sled in front of a small house near the fence that surrounded the Orc district. It was better kept than its neighbors in that its windows were all intact and the front yard was compressed gravel rather than mud. A low cold iron fence surrounded the yard with a sagging gate in front. Simon peered around as Sylvie opened the gate and approached the door. Satisfied that there was no immediate threat in sight, Simon followed. Hal remained with the sled, the D'Stang from the rear seat rack at his side.

Sylvie knocked hard at the front door.

"Tobit Fenreed," she called. "SED. Open up." There was no immediate answer, but Simon heard floorboards creak inside the house.

Sylvie knocked again. "Mr. Fenreed, it's urgent that we speak to you. Open the door."

A few seconds later, the door opened a crack and a bleary-eyed Orc peered out at them. He was of medium height and had the sharp nose and black hair of a Hyberian.

Sylvie pushed hard on the door, forcing the Orc to step back. She and Simon entered ignoring his inarticulate cries of protest. Simon drew his needler and checked left and right. The front door opened into a single room that ran the width of the house. A central hallway led toward the rear and what appeared to be a kitchen and a back door.

"Are you Tobit Fenreed?" asked Sylvie.

The Orc nodded, rubbing his eyes and shaking his head as if to clear it. He wore a short leather Hyberian kilt, rumpled hose and a sleeveless shirt that was stained with some dark green substance.

"You need to come with us," said Sylvie. "Get a coat and a change of clothing. We need to get you away from this house. Your life may be in danger."

"Who're you?" Fenreed asked, continuing to rub his eyes. "Why should I go with you?"

Sylvie showed him her badge. "I'm Ranger Graystorm and this is Sergeant Buckley of the Commonwealth Peacekeepers. Quickly, now. There's been a fire at the tavern and we're afraid you may be in danger."

Fereed stopped rubbing his eyes and gaped at Sylvie. "Fire? Is Gretl all good?"

"No time," said Simon. "Get a coat and anything else you need. We'll explain on the way." When the Orc still didn't move, Simon pointed the needler at him. "I don't have time to argue with you, Fenreed. You're coming with us upright or laid out, it makes no difference to me."

That got the Orc moving. He ran to a bedroom off the

central hallway, Sylvie right behind him, and stuffed a few clothes into a leather satchel. He took a coat from a peg by the door and looked at Simon. "Tell me Gretl is all good," he pleaded.

Simon felt a catch in his throat."In good time, Mr. Fenreed, but now we really have to go." He led the way, scanning the street. Hal stood by the sled, the D'Stang at his shoulder, scanning the houses next to them. With Fenreed between them, Simon and Sylvie hurried to the sled. Sylvie put Fenreed in the back as Simon went around to the driver's side. She and Simon got in while Hal covered them. Simon muttered the incantation to lift the sled and Hal jumped in just as they started forward.

"Where's Gretl?" asked Fenreed, becoming more agitated.

"I'm sorry, Mr. Fenreed," said Sylvie in her kindest voice. "We believe Gretl is dead. The fire at the tavern was no accident. We think Gretl and an Elf named Horace Silverlake were inside when it was attacked by a Fire mage. No one made it out of the fire."

The Orc recoiled as if Sylvie had slapped him. Then he slumped into the seat. "It's my fault. I should have left well enough alone. I just couldn't stand to see them kids burned and their folks not knowing what happened to them. Gretl told me I was a fool, but I didn't take heed."

"As a Ranger, I'm advising you to say no more until we can get you into protective custody." Sylvie glanced at Simon.

He nodded. "We'll take you somewhere safe. Then you can tell us what you know. All good?"

Fenreed only stared out the window, tears slowly rolling down his cheeks.

CHAPTER NINETEEN

Simon drove them past the tavern on their way to the district gate. Hal got out and spoke to the Fire Brigade incident commander. He learned that Gretl Ferneed had been confirmed among the dead as well as an unidentified male Elf.

Tobit Fenreed sat mute as Hal related this to Simon and Sylvie. They cleared the gate and Simon took them out of Portalis on the Talien highway. They hadn't discussed it but it seemed prudent to get Fenreed to the Borderlands station with all speed.

It was close to the twentieth hour by the time Simon pulled the sled into the nearly empty stables at Borderlands Station. Fenreed had been so quiet during the drive that Simon thought he'd fallen asleep. The Orc climbed out of the sled without a word and gazed around. Sylvie took his arm and led him through the security door to the stairs.

Fairborn and the day watch were long since gone. Sylvie

waved to a tall blond Elf woman who came over and greeted her warmly.

"Sylvie. Hamil told me you were back." She grasped Sylvie's hands.

"Good meeting, Genna," said Sylvie. "Are you the Watch Captain now?"

"Aye, and it looks like you've had a busy day," said Genna.

"That we have. Genna Silverthorn, meet Simon Buckley and Haldron Stonebender. This," Sylvie indicated Fenreed, "is Tobit Fenreed. He's a material witness in the case we're working. I'd like to put him in protective detention for a while until we can make sure he's safe to testify."

Silverthorn greeted Simon and Hal politely. She gave Fenreed a curt nod. "I think we can open up one of the VIP cells."

At the word 'cell' Fenreed looked up in alarm. Sylvie put a hand on his shoulder. "No locks," she said. "But a Ranger will be at the door all the time; to keep you safe."

"Safe from what?" asked Fenreed.

"Someone burned your wife and Horace Silverlake in their tavern because they knew too much," said Simon. "I'm thinking you have a good idea who did that and why. That person has to answer for those deaths, and for the deaths of four young children."

Fenreed looked down at the mention of the children. "I didn't know he was going to do that."

"Who, Tobit?" Sylvie asked gently. "Who killed the children?"

"I didn't see it," whispered Fenreed. "I know he done it, but I didn't actually see."

"See who," asked Simon.

"The *Syr*, he told his gardener to take the bundles to the burn pit. 'Don't worry what's in them', says he. 'Just scraps from the spring lamb slaughter', says he. But I was loading the laundry and I seen the little foot of that girl and

I knew."

"And you put them in the laundry sledge and took them to Cymbeline," said Simon.

Fenreed swallowed hard. "I took them home. They deserved to go home."

"Who was the *Syr?*" asked Sylvie. "Lindenfield?"

"No," Fenreed shook his head. "It were *Syr* Dalien. *Syr* Gheran Dalien of Elm Gables. He and his Lady wife been the *Syr* and *Dania* there for near on sixty years. Always thought them proper High Folk until I found them kids. I knew nobody in these parts would ever think ill of them, so I didn't tell, except to Gretl. Horace Silverlake like as not knew something, as he was the one sold the indentures to *Syr* Gheran. And now they's both dead and it's my fault."

"No." Sylvie patted his shoulder. "You did nothing wrong. But we need to make sure nothing happens to you as well. Ranger Silverthorn is going to have one of her people show you to a place where you can rest. If you need anything, just ask."

Silverthorn waved one of the junior Rangers over and whispered some quick instructions. Simon tried not to notice the doubtful look the Ranger gave Fenreed. To be fair, he was properly polite to the Orc as he led him away.

"What do you know about Gheran Dalien?" Simon asked Silverthorn.

"He's well liked in the district, though not originally from around here. He lived in the Commonwealth for a time, up near Fastnet, I think. Married his wife there. Moved here about sixty years ago when his uncle, the original *Syr* Dalien passed into the Green Dream. He's been a good master by all accounts, more liberal than most, in truth. Maybe because his wife is Human."

"*Dania* Dalien is Human?" Simon stiffened.

"Oh, aye," said Silverthorn. "I suspect she's as much as half Elf, though. She's over eighty but I'm told she still looks no more than half that age."

Hal stroked his beard. He'd said nothing since they had left Portalis. He and Simon exchanged a look.

"Possible," Hal said. He looked at Silverthorn. "Is this Gheran Dalien a Fire mage?"

"Any High Elf can do basic magic, but more complex spells require training," said Silverthorn. "If he's a mage, he hasn't let it be known."

Sylvie looked from Simon to Hal. "Just because his wife is Human . . ."

Simon held up a hand. "I don't care. We have four dead children. We have the sledge and we have Fenreed. All the evidence points to the Havens, and now to Elm Gables. If it isn't Dalien, then it's someone close to that estate."

"You can't believe that a High Elf, a *Syr* of the Council, would have anything to do with kidnap and murder," protested Silverthorn.

Simon drew himself up. "I saw a Fire mage, an Elf, cast the spell that torched that tavern and killed Gretl Fenreed. I saw his face. I'll know him if I see him again. If it was Dalien, I'll want him detained to answer for it."

"My Rangers and I know our duties, sir." Silverthorn's voice was iron hard. She turned to Sylvie. "Good meeting, Sylvie. You know where the billets are. I must get back to work."

Hal touched Sylvie's arm. "Let's go find Liam, lass."

Together they found Liam in a small office surrounded by sheets of flimsy paper. He looked up as they came in and grinned.

"Simon, Hal, Sylvie," he greeted them in turn. "I've got a half dozen names linked to large purchases of gold in the last six months. How did it go up in the city?"

Simon filled him in on the fire, and on what Tobit Fenreed had just told them. "But I doubt they'll issue a writ for a search of the estate on the word of an Orc," said Simon. "What have you found?"

"Dalien?" Liam sifted through his papers. "Here he is. I

"But why, *Syr* Gheran?" asked Sylvie, laying a hand on his shoulder. "Why? Your wife is Human. You must have known it couldn't last."

"I can't lose her," Dalien said through tears. "Sixty-three years together. We share *ghiras.* So much of my self is tied to her, I'm afraid of what will happen when she dies. I can't live without her."

Simon lowered his needler and Sylvie reached out, turning Dalien to face the wall. "Place your hands behind you, *Syr* Gheran," she said, taking a pair of manacles from her pouch.

"Please," said Dalien. "Let me see my wife unfettered. I'll go with you, in the manacles if you wish. But allow me the dignity of talking to my wife without chains on my wrists. I would embrace her one last time."

Sylvie looked at Simon, who nodded.

"Very well," Sylvie said.

Dalien moved to pick up his walking stick, but Simon stopped him with a twitch of the needler.

"No, that stays here," said Simon. "And I'll have that chain as well; and the aquamarine ring on your left hand."

Dalien removed the chain and the ring, handing them to Simon with a wry smile. "You are a suspicious man."

"I'm a careful man," answered Simon. He motioned with the needler toward the stairway.

Dalien led them up the staircase to a wide second floor hallway and down to a room on the end. He opened the door and they stepped into a large, airy bedchamber. Tall windows overlooked the meadow below. Through them, Simon could see Hal leaning against the fender of their sled, watching the house. Dalien noted him as well.

Alise sat at a vanity next to a canopied bed, adjusting the collar of a high-necked gown. Melisa, the Orc maid stood next to her, a scarf in her hands. Dalien pointed to the door and the maid curtsied and left the room.

"May I have a moment with my wife, please," he asked

Sylvie. "As you can see, there is no other door and the widows are watched by your man below."

Sylvie hesitated for a moment. "Very well. We'll be in the hall, but the door stays open." She motioned to Simon who followed reluctantly.

Simon turned as they crossed the threshold and held his needler at the ready. Dalien bent and whispered in his wife's ear. She rose and turned to embrace him. He glanced back over his shoulder at Simon, a sad smile on his lips. He gave a small shake of his head and the door swung shut.

Simon slammed into the door with his shoulder, which only resulted in pain shooting down his arm. Sylvie drew her rapier as Simon stood back and gathered himself to kick at the door where the handle met the frame. He stopped as a burning pain ran down his spine.

"Sylvie, get down!" he shouted, diving to his left and pushing her to the floor.

The door splintered and started to fold inward. A piece the size of his head crumbled to dust and seemed to be sucked away. The world stopped for a brief second then the door and most of the room exploded into searing white flame. Heat blistered the backs of his legs. The wall to his right protected them from the inferno for the time being but it was already beginning to smoke.

"Out!" Simon shouted. "Downstairs; get everyone outside."

Sylvie struggled to her feet and limped down the hall, keeping to the wall. Simon peered into the room but was driven back by another blast of heat. He turned and followed Sylvie.

By the time they reached the ground floor, Nistor and Melisa were herding the kitchen help and other servants out the front door.

"Is there anyone else in the house?" Simon asked.

"No one, sir," the Orc said. "But the *Syr* and *Dania*?"

Simon shook his head. Nistor started toward the stairs,

but Simon grabbed his shoulder and held him back.

"This was your Master's doing," said Simon. "I'll not have anyone else harmed by it."

Together they joined the small crowd outside. Simon looked up at the house. The entire south wing was now ablaze, pouring thick smoke into the late morning sky. *How?* thought Simon. *I took his ring, his gold and his cane. How did he cast a spell that powerful? Wait, Alise wore a gold comb with blue stones, aquamarine maybe. And I'll wager the panels on that door were rowan.*

Sylvie was there, at his side, staring up at the flames.

"Why?" he asked.

"He didn't just want to embrace her one last time." Her voice was filled with sadness. "He wanted to take her with him the only way he could. His obsession with her was too strong."

"What was it the *demilia*, Forsaka, said?" Simon mused. "Someone whose need was great bonded to one who is willing to commit any act to meet it?" He felt Sylvie shiver next to him. He put his arm around her. She stiffened momentarily, then leaned against him.

"His need was as great as hers," she whispered.

CHAPTER TWENTY

By the time the Fire Brigade arrived, there was little left of the south wing of the house. The fire didn't spread beyond the central foyer but appeared to burn itself out. Sylvie summoned the team leader of the detention sledge and instructed them to stand down and return to Borderlands Station. Simon noted that she didn't tell them about Dalien and his lady.

The ride back to the station passed in silence. Even Hal had nothing to say. Despite Sylvie withholding any description of the fire, word spread on the Fire Brigade FS net. Summerfield was waiting for them at Borderlands Station.

"Graystorm. Buckley." Summerfield addressed them as the team entered the squad room. "Watch Captain's office, now. The rest of you, stand by until I call for you."

Hamil Fairborn edged past Simon as they passed each other at the entrance to the small office in the southwest corner of the squad room. Fairborn was the day Watch Captain, nearing the end of his shift. Simon noticed Genna Silvertorn looking on with barely concealed glee.

Sylvie entered right behind Simon and they stood side by side in front of Fairborn's now vacant desk. Summerfield came in a minute later and stood behind the desk. Sylvie snapped to attention and Simon managed a semblance of it. *Summerfield wasn't HIS commander, but damn, the man had presence.*

"A *Syr* of the Council is dead," said Summerfield. "Burned in a fire the incident commander says was set by a Fire mage. Your team was there. Explain."

"My mage was in the meadow, too far away to have cast the immolation spell," said Simon stiffly. "Sylvie and I were nearly killed by Dalien's casting." He went on to describe the encounter with Dalien and his suicide.

"You're certain that's what it was?"

"I saw the look he gave me before the door slammed."

Sylvie spoke up. "It was his *ghiras*. He loved her deeply. When her mind began to go, he became desperate. He couldn't be parted from her and stay sane."

Summerfield's shoulders slumped at the mention of *ghiras*. "And the writ of search? I assume you found evidence linking Dalien to the children if you detained him."

"Fenreed witnessed Dalien telling his gardener to dispose of the remains in the estate burn pit." Simon held up a hand when Summerfield began to object. "I know he's an Orc. But I didn't need that. I saw Dalien cast the Fire spell that killed Fenreed's wife and Horace Silverlake, the two people who could tie him to the auction barn. I detained him for those murders."

"You have some corroboration? Did anyone else see this?" asked Summerfield.

Simon bristled. "I'm no Orc."

Summerfield shook his head. "No, but we're talking about a *Syr* of the Council. The Traditionalists will have my head and Sylvie's and make sure you never come back to the Havens again if this case isn't sewn up tighter than a Dwarf's purse."

Simon smiled in spite of himself at the old adage. "Have your forensics people do an aural screen on the tavern and house at Elm Gables. They'll match. The same mage cast both spells. The aura won't match mine, Liam's or Hal's. I assume Sylvie needs no such vindication."

Summerfield's face twitched at the jab. "We'll run hers as well. What about the connection to the Commonwealth? Do we know how those children came to be at Elm Gables?"

"Not precisely." Simon grew thoughtful. "I know Dalien bought their indentures from Horace Silverlake at the auction. I can connect both Silverlake cousins to Sailesh Grimsley and Grimsley to Biran Stillwater. I need to speak with Hiramis Silverlake again. Now that his cousin is dead, he's looking at the gallows unless he gives us Grimsley and the rest of the network."

"But can you give me proof I can take to the Council that Dalien bought those children from Silverlake and killed them in some Blood ritual to keep his wife alive?"

"No," said Simon. "I can give you proof that he killed Gretl Fenreed and Horace Silverlake. The rest is circumstantial."

Summerfield sat down behind the desk. "It will have to be enough, I suppose. I know the traffic in illegal indentures goes higher than Dalien. If anything, he was just a convenient buyer. I had hoped this case would give me a lever to push; that Dalien would give me names or a hook to shut this trade down once and for all."

"Do you think he knew anyone involved besides Silverlake?" asked Sylvie. "He made it sound like Silverlake was his only contact with the auctions."

Summerfield rubbed the middle of his forehead. "Perhaps not. He must have recognized some of the other bidders. They were his neighbors, after all."

"The auctions themselves weren't illegal here in the

Havens," said Simon.

"No, more's the pity," answered Summerfield. "But if the indentures weren't valid, or were forged, we'd have a case."

"The case is back in the Commonwealth. And we have Grimsley and the other Silverlake in custody."

"For now," said Summerfield.

"Meaning?"

"Meaning I have heard disturbing rumors about the death of Biran Stillwater and your involvement in it."

"Have you gotten official word from my Captain?" asked Simon.

"No," admitted Summerfield. "The information is from other sources."

"George Latham?" Sylvie asked. Summerfield gave her a sharp look. "Dalien knew about Simon and the investigation over Stillwater. He said George Latham was his source."

Summerfield exhaled. "That's . . . troublesome."

"Troublesome?" said Simon. "That's what you call it? How long has Latham been working for the Rangers?"

"Just since the Flandyrs affair. And he's not working for us. He's working for King Thorston."

"How's that?"

"His Majesty needed a back channel to the Rangers that didn't involve Traditionalist diplomats and the Steward," said Summerfield "He'd pass us information the Palace thought we would find useful, and we'd reciprocate. So, yes, it's troublesome that he'd be in communication with Dalien."

"Princess Rebeka engaged Latham to represent Hiramis Silverlake," said Simon. "Maybe it wasn't Dalien, but Horace Silverlake that Latham spoke to. It might have been advocate – client stuff, not diplomatic stuff."

"I hope to the gods you're right." Summerfield sat forward. "Dalien wasn't in the Steward's inner circle, but his position on the Council was tenuous. If Latham or Silverlake told him anything of substance, we have to assume the Steward knows it, too."

Summerfield gave them a wave of dismissal and they left the office. The Senior Ranger shouted for an aide and began giving orders for handling the scene at Elm Gables, making it officially a crime scene rather than a routine fire. Sylvie crossed the squad room and spoke briefly with Fairborn. Simon motioned Hal and Liam over.

"We need to get back to the Commonwealth," said Simon. "This side of the Border is a dead end now, and may get unhealthy for us before long. Some of Summerfield's forensic people will get aural screens from all of us, after which we should be free to go."

"What about Sylvie, lad?" asked Hal.

"I don't know. This is her beat and she's in Summerfield's chain of command. At the least she'll be stuck until the reports are all filed. Hopefully they won't keep her here pending an inquest. There aren't any charges to file. Silverlake's partners in the auction ring are too well connected to let that happen, even if we could identify them."

Sylvie came over and joined them. "I'm on desk duty until all the reports are in. I convinced Hamil that it wouldn't be efficient to keep me here until the formal inquest when there's still a case to pursue on the other side of the Border. He'll convince Summerfield."

"How long will all that take?" asked Simon.

"A day or so for the formal reports. Likely another week until the inquest is even scheduled." She gave his arm a gentle squeeze. "Go back home, love. I'll join you as soon as I can."

"We'll be at the hotel in West Faring for a day or so taking care of the paperwork on Grimsley and filing out reports on our sled run through town. I imagine Sergeant Utzler is neck deep by now and none too happy with me for leaving him the mess."

"I'll join you there if I can close this out by tomorrow,

but I'll likely need to be back for the inquest."

Simon smiled. "It's the job. We both knew that going in."

She touched his cheek with her palm before turning back to the squad room and the waiting reports.

Simon, Hal and Liam arrived in West Faring just after dark. Liam and Hal went down into town in search of a decent tavern, but Simon was too tired for a night out. He fell into bed as soon as his teammates left.

His dreams were of Sylvie. Lately, when they were apart, he'd felt her presence in his dreams more and more often, like he had once felt Alira; not as an image of herself but as a background presence, like the lover standing behind you who you can sense but not feel. This night Sylvie's presence seemed tinged with sadness and his dreams where vague images of overcast melancholy vistas.

He awoke at dawn, rested but troubled. He supposed it had to do with Dalien's suicide and the hole it left in both his and Summerfield's investigations. He knew in his heart that Dalien had killed those children and a part of him wanted to understand why, but despite Sylvie's explanation, it didn't make sense to him. Deep abiding love he thought he could understand. But love that degenerated into madness? Could the same thing happen to Sylvie? He thrust the thought aside.

It also troubled him that he was not upset by the death of Alise Dalien. It had not been her choice, but perhaps it would have been the choice she'd have made if she understood what her husband had done. Now no one would know.

Simon met Hal and Liam in the hotel dining room, Hal sipping strong tea and Liam wolfing down eggs and smoked fish.

"Good news, Boss," said Liam. "Kermal and Jack have a lead on Kronska. Looks like he went to ground in an old rope warehouse near the Prince Henrik Bridge."

Hal sipped his tea. "Aye. We need to clear things up here

and get back to the House. You sure Utzler can't handle things himself?"

Simon sat and poured coffee from a pot in the center of the table.

"He's a good Keeper, Hal. He did right by us. He's earned some help."

"Good Keeper should be able to handle a little thing like a sled run and prisoner transfer," grumbled Hal. "But I suppose you won't let it go, so let's get it over with." His smile gave the lie to his grumpy tone.

Hal and Simon met Utzler at the Civil Patrol station near the North gate. The grizzled Keeper greeted them with a broad smile and a handshake. "Wasn't sure you'd come by," he said. "Th' report on your Orc's arrest is done, just needs a sign-off. Your Wycliffe House sent a wagon down, picked the scab up yest'day. What's he pinched for, if y'don't mind me askin'?"

"Kidnap and selling false indentures on the other side of the Border," said Simon. "The rangers are working that side."

Utzler nodded. "Bad business. We stopped a sledge load of Orcs just last week bein' hauled West. Most of 'em Azeri with no clue what they were headin' to. Couldn't do much. They'd been hoodwinked good an' proper an' only two got out when our advocates gave them th' chance. Poor sods."

"All adults?" asked Simon.

"Oh, aye," said Utzler. "We know some kids are in th' sledges sometimes, but we've not found any in th' past year or so. The transporters 'ave gotten wise an' bypass West Faring."

"Grimsley was one of the worst. He bought children from a gang leader named Stillwater, up in Cymbeline. Did that name ever pop up when you stopped these sledges?"

"Aye, we know of Biran Stillwater," said Utzler. "But Cymbeline's way outside my beat. Not much I could do."

"You've done a lot already. Thanks."

but sloppy; like the Fire mage didn't care how it looked or how much trace aura he left behind."

"Did anyone get out?" asked Simon.

"Didn't know there was anyone in there," Smithington answered. "Old building, nowhere near up to code. The fire started in the center core of the warehouse, explosive combustion. If there was anyone in there and they weren't right next to a door, they'd have been dead before they knew what hit them."

"No one in or out after fourth," said Jack. "Kronska was in there with at least two of his closest boyos."

"So at least three dead." Simon watched the dark plume of smoke still rising over what remained of the warehouse..

"Why do we care?" asked Jack. "Good riddance if you ask me."

"I've no love for Nose Kronska," said Simon. "But this game is wider than a small time gang captain trying to corner the jolt trade. With both Stillwater and Kronska gone, who benefits? Who set this up? The Brigades? Some other gang?"

"The Brigades," said Jack. "They've had a foothold in the drug trade, but only at low levels."

"Logical, but since we took down Barsaka, they haven't had the leadership or the muscle to enforce a major move into the Hollows." Simon rubbed his chin, thinking. "For now, it's our only lead. See what you can learn from the Civil Patrol Keepers on the Hollows beat. Someone knows who hit Kronska. Until we find that out, we're groping in the dark."

The summoning tone of Simon's mirror interrupted them. He took it out and swiped it on.

"Where are you, Boss?" Liam asked. "Kermal and I are here at the House with four of Lillihammers's guys. We just got word that the warehouse is afire."

"I'm with Jack at the scene. I want you and Kermal down here. Give the forensics team a heads up as well. The

Fire commander says this is arson. Kronska and his crew were inside which puts this in our laps. I want a complete aural analysis and forensic search of the scene."

"Aye," said Liam. "We're on our way."

Simon turned to Smithington. "How long before my guys can get in there?"

The Water mage surveyed the progress of his team. "Fire's almost knocked down, but the inside will be hot for the rest of the day. And we'll need to check the stability of any remaining structure. Like as not, tomorrow at the earliest."

"Did you get that, Liam?" Simon asked.

"Got it. I'll give Evarts a call but tell him we'll be limited to the perimeter until the place cools down. Aster out."

Simon put the mirror back in his pocket. Jack took his leave to stand down the surveillance team and send them back to their regular duties. Simon slumped against the side of his Oxley.

What now? Without Kronska I've got nothing but my word against Killian's. And he filed the complaint. All the IG is going to see is that I went to Lily's first with most of my team. I vetted the meeting. Even if there's no evidence, I'll be the one on suspension.

Liam and Kermal drove up behind him in a patrol sled a few minutes later as he was still mulling it over. The Fire Brigade mages had plenty of water to work with and had nearly extinguished the blaze. Only a few hot spots remained in the smoking ruins. The roof and three of the four walls had collapsed into the cellar leaving only mounds of ash, charred timbers and twisted metal framing. If there were bodies in there, they were deep in the debris.

Simon greeted his teammates, everyone subdued by the turn of events. Both Liam and Kermal understood the potential fallout with Kronska's death, not just to Simon's career but also to the Hollows. The power vacuum created by both Stillwater and Kronska being eliminated within

CHAPTER TWENTY-TWO

Simon tried Liam's mirror again but got no response. He checked with Hal, but Liam hadn't contacted him either.

"I'm getting worried, Hal," said Simon. "This isn't like Liam. Have Jack go around and check his flat. I'll contact Harold and see if he's been to the Palace."

"Want me to put out an alert with Lillihammer's boys on the day shift?"

"Not yet, but if he doesn't report in by end of watch, do it."

He closed the connection. He changed his shirt and hose before leaving to meet Kermal. As he picked up his mirror from the nightstand, he noticed a new text on the message scroll. It was from Liam.

"Boss, sorry about vanishing. It's important. Please meet me. Lily's 23rd hour. Important. Will explain."

Simon summoned Liam's mirror, but the spell flipped to the message scroll again. "Damn it, Liam. What the hells kind of game are you playing?"

He stuck the mirror in his pocket and left the flat.

Kermal was waiting for him in the common room at Lily's. The room was not crowded this early in the evening and most of the other patrons clustered around the bar. Kermal sat at the back booth where Kronska had been the night Stillwater was killed. He was dressed in his best uniform, freshly pressed with starched shirt and a mirror shine on his boots.

Simon glanced down at his own rumpled uniform and stained boots. Kermal noticed and smiled.

"No worries, Sarge," he said. "The people we're going to see won't care."

"So you say," said Simon ruefully.

"I have to show respect to these men. You're Human and my boss. They expect you to be arrogant and superior."

"And casually rude?"

Kermal grimaced. "They're Orcs in a Human world. They expect no respect from you."

Simon was taken aback by this casual expectation. He'd always shown respect, even deference, to Orc leaders like Lily, Gran Swampwater, and even that *demilvosk* shaman Forsaka. That they'd feel that way about Elves and Dwarves he could understand. But didn't the Accords mean anything? *Are we really that much like the others? If Killian is any example, perhaps we are.*

"So when can we expect this guide?" Simon changed the subject.

"Any minute." Kermal checked his timepiece. "It's just now quarter 'til."

As if on cue, the tavern doors opened and a small Orc woman stepped in. Simon glanced at her then stopped and stared as she approached. She was petite, slim and well proportioned with long jet-black hair. Her skin was the color of cinnamon and her almond shaped eyes a brilliant green. Her features were more Elven than Orcish, but there was no mistaking her race. Serpent tattoos wound around her exposed forearms and peeked out from under her low collared shirt. She wore a camel hair vest and green riding trousers bloused over rough boots.

"You are Simon Buckley," she said in Azeri accented Common Speech.

Simon nodded.

"You and the *Hagashi* will follow me." She turned toward the door without awaiting an answer.

Kermal glared at her, but said nothing as he stood and followed. Simon fell in beside him.

"*Hagashi*?" Simon whispered as they reached the street.

"It's an insult. It means someone who's pretending to be something he's not."

The woman walked south, across Knacker Street, at a brisk walk. Simon and Kermal hurried to keep up. After a couple of blocks she turned right into a warren of alleys and narrow streets that ran along the canal and behind the backs of the buildings fronting the main street. A confusing series of twists and turns brought them to a blind alley that ended at a red door.

The afternoon was edging into twilight and the alley was already in deep shadow, almost as dark as full night. Simon glanced about and laid a hand on the hilt of his saber. The woman noticed and gave a small shake of her head. She rapped at the door, which opened almost immediately. She stood aside and indicated that they should enter.

Simon and Kermal stepped into a small anteroom and the door closed behind them. Facing them stood a massive Orc, half a head taller than Simon and twice as broad. He was dressed in a modern business suit, well tailored and expensive looking. To his left a smaller Orc held a D'Stang lightweight bolt thrower that he pointed in their general direction.

"I am Holf, security for these elders. I'm going to search your person for concealed weapons," the big Orc said in a surprisingly pleasant voice. "Raise your arms"

Simon and Kermal complied and the Orc quickly and efficiently searched them. He took Simon's needler, ejected the magazine and cleared the spring chamber then handed it back. He slid the Gallinberg out of its sheath for a few inches, examined the exposed part of the blade and then slid it home again. He took Kermal's sidearm but allowed him to keep his short sword. Search complete, Holf stood aside and gestured to a round table on the other side of a narrow but richly appointed room. Five elderly looking Orcs sat around the table, which was covered by a white tablecloth and set for tea. Several of the Orcs sipped from small porcelain cups. A large silver teakettle dominated the center of the table. Trays of almonds, olives, savory meats and sliced cucumber lay scattered about.

Simon and Kermal approached them slowly. "These people are very dangerous and very suspicious," whispered Kermal. "Take it slow. Make no sudden moves. Accept tea and wait for one of them to ask you who you know. Give them my name and my father's name. Be polite and respectful, but also ready to kill everyone here if it goes sideways."

Simon nodded and looked at each of the Orcs in turn. They ranged in age from merely old to truly ancient. Tattoos wound around narrow pale arms and thin necks: Serpent, Wind, Fish, Wolf, Bear, and Rat. Conspicuously absent was Ox Clan. The oldest looking Orc sat unmoving in a chair directly across from the door. Simon would have thought him dead, but noticed the slow rise and fall of his chest. His eyes were closed, asleep perhaps? As Simon turned, he noticed one hooded eye slit open slightly to follow him.

He stopped when he saw the red robed Orc sitting closest to the door. Kalmish Forsaka, the *demilia* he and Sylvie had interviewed, looked up at him with an amused smile.

"Peace, Sergeant Buckley," he said. "You have been

summoned by the Cabal. Who do you know that gives you introduction to our circle?"

"Kermal Brackenville, son of Hasfal," said Simon. Then he added, "And Kalmish Forsaka, *demilvosk* and shopkeeper."

Forsaka smiled and shifted in his seat. He extended a hand toward the vacant chairs. "Sit and take tea with us."

Simon noted the heavy gold bracer around the *demilvosk's* wrist as he pulled out the indicated chair and sat. Kermal remained standing, almost at attention, at his back.

Forsaka poured tea from the ornate kettle and set the tiny porcelain cup before Simon. He picked up his own cup and held it up in a gesture of salute. Simon returned it and they both drank.

"I won't introduce my colleagues." Forsaka set down his tea cup. "Their names would mean nothing to you. I will express their appreciation for the capture of Sailesh Grimsley and Hiramis Silverlake. The trade in children had become an intolerable burden on our people."

"You burned Biran Stillwater for it," said Simon. "You were the mage Killian spoke to in the alley. Why didn't you take care of Grimsley and Silverlake yourself?"

Simon felt Kermal stiffen behind him. Several of the Orcs at the table frowned, but Forsaka waved a hand and laughed. "Direct and fearless. I do like you, Simon Buckley. To answer your question, we rarely act so directly and never against Humans or Elves, at least not here in the Commonwealth. Orcs killing Orcs never gets much official attention, but an Orc killing a Human or an Elf? Especially one with Royal connections? That would raise questions we don't welcome."

He reached into the folds of his red robe and drew out a sheaf of papers bound with string. "Here you'll find records of Francis Killian's meetings with Farsk Kronska. Dates, times and witnesses who will testify that they plotted to kill

Stillwater and take over his organization. Kronska was to take over the drug trade and Killian would look the other way. In return, Kronska would guarantee a peace of sorts in the Hollows and inform Killian of other gang related activities so that his team could look good to his superiors."

Simon eyed the papers but didn't pick them up. "But you cast the spell that killed Stillwater, correct."

"Killian needed to appear blameless. I facilitated his plan."

"Then why are you giving me this?" Simon indicated the sheaf of papers. "Why betray Killian? He could weasel on you for the murder of Stillwater."

"He could, but he will not. He has a family to protect." Forsaka's tone was cold, but casual, as if this simple statement carried none of the threat it implied.

"But why burn Kronska and betray Killian after going to the trouble of setting them up?"

Forsaka sat upright. "We did not kill Kronska. That was Killian's doing, and will be his undoing."

Simon rubbed his chin, puzzled. "Killian didn't kill Kronska. He's no mage and he doesn't have a Fire mage on his team."

Forsaka waved a dismissive hand. "Professionals are easily hired for that work."

"But the arson was amateurish," said Simon. "No attempt to make it look accidental and no effort to conceal the mage's aura."

"And yet you accuse me?" said Forsaka mildly. "You know that had I set that fire it would look spontaneous and even the best forensic mage wouldn't know better." The Orc pushed the papers toward Simon. "Take this. You'll need it to clear yourself and resume your real duties. Kronska's death will touch off a power struggle here in the Hollows. It will be bad for business. You'll need to act quickly to keep it contained."

"Why don't you and your colleagues here fix it?" Simon

left the papers on the table between them. "You could hand pick another Kronska and stop the chaos."

"We don't really care who manages the trade. It's bad for our people but at least it's contained. Besides, there is no one with enough steel to lead yet." Forsaka made a slight gesture to the other Orcs. "We are merely a group of interested elders. We work behind the scenes to further larger ends for our people. Kronska's death benefits no one. Killian is wrong if he thinks this will end the drug trade."

"But Killian didn't . . . " Simon paled and stopped speaking as he realized that Killian would have known the futility of killing Kronska. And he also realized who would not have understood that.

Forsaka looked at him expectantly. Simon nodded and picked up the sheaf of papers. He drained the dregs of tea from his cup and set it upside down on the table.

"By your leave," said Simon, rising from the table. "Come on, Kermal. We're done here."

Kermal didn't move and after a few steps, Simon turned and looked back.

"Kermal?"

The Half-Orc armorer smiled sadly and removed the lanyard and badge from his shoulder. He held them out to Simon. "Sorry, Simon. I need to stay. Tell the rest of the team, especially Jack and Liam, that I was honored to work with them."

"Kermal, what the hells are you doing?"

"*Kul ghiras annan sarngal*," said Kermal with a rueful smile. "I'm needed here."

"Mr. Brackenville will assume his father's duties," said Forsaka.

Simon glanced from Forsaka to Kermal. "As an assassin?"

"Hopefully it won't come to that," said Kermal. "But I can't turn my back and walk away. I can't be a good *Hargashi* anymore. Not when innocent people will start dying because of a gang war. I can help stop that, but not if I'm bound by the badge."

"The badge is what separates us from the criminals," said Simon. "Without it, and the rules it makes us follow, we're no better than the Killians and Kronskas of the world."

"And what am I?" asked Kermal. "Working on your team was the first time I was taken seriously in five years on the job. Always the token Orc or the errand boy. Never a 'real' Keeper. Do you think I'll ever make Sergeant? Or get my own team to lead?" He held out a hand to Simon. "I don't want us to part as enemies, Simon. But this is the Path I've been shown. It's the one I have to follow."

Simon took his hand and held it. "Don't do this, Kermal. I can't look the other way if you break the law, even in the name of some greater good."

"I know that Simon." He grinned. "I wouldn't expect anything else. Try to explain to the rest of the team. Please?"

"Sure." Simon released Kermal's hand, took the badge and lanyard from him, and left the room. The beautiful Orc woman was waiting for him outside the red door. She led him back to Canal Street and then disappeared into the evening traffic.

Simon walked slowly back to Lily's. He gripped Kermal's badge and lanyard, wondering if there was anything else he could have said. *Is it my fault? I thought I was doing the right thing in treating him like any other team member. I should have tried harder to see things from his view point. Did I assign him jobs based more on his race than I should have?* Whatever Kermal's reasons, Simon decided he couldn't have done things any differently. *I hope he knows what he's doing, because there will be no coming back.*

He checked his timepiece again. Barely half past seventh. Too soon to wait in Lily's place for Liam, and the temptation to drink too much might be too strong. He needed to get the evidence from Forsaka to a safe place in any event. He found his Oxley and drove back to Wycliffe House.

Hal had left a note on his desk – no news from upstairs and no word from Liam. He asked Simon to summon his mirror when there was anything to report.

Simon slumped behind his desk, not wanting to speak to anyone at the moment. He opened the sheaf of papers and began to review them. As Forsaka had promised, they contained details of a series of meetings between Kronska and Killian. There were specific dates, locations and names of witnesses along with their contact information. Enough to clear Simon and potentially put Killian in prison for abuse of his authority and conspiracy to murder Stillwater. He took images of each page with his mirror and time logged them. Then he sealed the papers in a large envelope and addressed it to Captain Axhart. He stood intending to take the package upstairs and leave it in Axhart's office.

"I hope that's for me," said a voice from his right. Simon turned to see Axhart himself standing in the doorway.

"Yes, sir," said Simon. "It is. How did you know?"

"I got word from what I'll call an anonymous source that Frank Killian knew more about Stillwater's death than he's been saying; and that you had evidence to prove it." Axhart looked at the envelope in Simon's hand. "I assume that's it."

"Yes sir. Dates, places, and names of witnesses." Simon handed him the envelope. "I'm told that Frank won't dispute it."

"Do I want to be knowing how you got this?"

"No sir," said Simon with a slight smile. "Not unless it's critical. Do I need to know your anonymous source?"

Axhart laughed. "Point taken. Needless to say, this kills that IG complaint. You and your team have free rein to continue your investigation."

"The case is just about wrapped, Captain. At least on this side of the Border. Grimsley and Silverlake are in custody. The children have been identified and families informed where they could be found. The situation in the

Havens is a bit muddier." He outlined the events in Portalis and at Elm Gables.

"Is there any doubt about Dalien being the one who killed the children?"

"No, he as much as confessed before he killed himself. But the rest of the child smuggling network on that side of the border is still intact. They could find another willing partner over here and restart the operation."

"I know, but if Rulanis Summerfield can't shut them down, there's little we can do."

"But what if the King were to let the Steward know that this goes all the way up to his closest advisors," said Simon.

Axhart held up his hand. "Without proof, His Majesty isn't likely to make accusations like that. And given Tintagel's response to the Flandyrs case, do you really think they'll take action over some orphaned Orc children?"

Simon sighed. "No sir. Maybe Kermal is right."

"What's that?" asked Axhart. "What's Brackenville got to do with this?"

Simon laid the badge and lanyard on the desk. "He's resigned from the force, sir. He says he can be more help to his people if he's not restrained by the badge."

"Hells," said Axhart. "That's unfortunate. We had high hopes for him. If this has anything to do with Stonebender's stupid bigotry, I'll bust him to street patrol."

"No, sir. Hal had some trouble at first, but he came around. And Kermal and Jack became close. They worked well together."

"Then why?" asked Axhart.

"I don't know for sure, sir," said Simon. "Maybe the Force isn't ready for Orc Keepers. Maybe he got tired of being the test case for all of his people. Or maybe spirit really does follow the blood."

That last caused Axhart to look sharply at Simon. "You're sure he acted on his own free will? That it wasn't pressure from a table full of old men?"

"They may have had something to do with it, but I'm convinced Kermal believes he's doing the right thing."

Axhart picked up the badge. "So be it," he said with a trace of sadness. "I'll be needing to see you in my office tomorrow, midday. Have your reports on the Havens case ready by then. And think about replacement armorers for the team." With that, he turned and left the office.

Simon spent the next several hours trying to work. He polished the reports on their findings in the Havens. He tried to review case law regarding arson with accidental or intentional death and went over the rules of evidence for an arrest based on aural analysis. By twenty-second hour he was tired, bleary eyed and depressed.

He strapped on his sword belt, saber, and the holster for his needler. He smoothed some of the rumples out of his jacket and looped the lanyard with his badge through the shoulder strap. Then he descended the stairs to the stables and went to his Oxley. After a minutes thought, he turned and went to the stable master to check out an official sled.

CHAPTER TWENTY-THREE

By twenty-third hour he was sitting outside Lily's. He took several deep breaths, struggling to control a sudden surge of anger at Liam. *It'll do no good to go roaring in there and lay into Liam for jeopardizing the entire team and his career.* He told himself for the third time. *He's young. His passion has gotten the better of him.*

After a couple of minutes he climbed out of the sled and strode into the tavern. The common room was crowded and dozens of eyes looked his way as he crossed to the bar. Conversation buzzed around him, but the tone was more curious than hostile. He found Liam waiting for him at the end of the bar near the doors to the kitchen. The Fire mage looked haggard but determined. Simon would have preferred contrition.

"Simon," said Liam gravely. "Thank you for coming."

"You didn't give me much choice, Liam. What I should do is put you on suspension and call a disciplinary hearing.

Stenson. I know you want to protect her, but we can't let her off just because of who she is. That's the way thing work in Tintagel. Orc children are being sold into virtual slavery because the people doing it are connected to the Steward. We can't let that happen here."

"She's still my charge, Simon," said Harold, his voice breaking. "I swore an oath to protect her with my life."

Simon reached out and touched the insignia of the Royal Security Service sewn to Harold's left breast pocket. "We both swore an oath to the King and Commonwealth. The law, Stenson. Either it means something or it means nothing."

Harold shook his head. "This is a personal duty, not an ideal. She's as much as my own daughter. I can't abandon her."

"You've already failed her," growled Simon. "Where were you when all this went on? I saw the limo that brought her down here. Did you drive it? Should I be detaining you as an accomplice?"

"Watch yourself, Buckley," Harold warned, dropping his hand to the butt of his needler.

"Stop, Stenson," said Rebeka. "This is my sin." She looked up at Simon. "Yes, Sergeant Buckley. I understand the caution. Stenson wasn't on duty. I convinced one of his men to drive for me. He didn't know until today about the fires." She held out her hands, expecting him to place her in manacles.

"Who drove for you, Highness?" Harold asked.

"I won't tell you that, Stenson," she replied. "I promised him my protection and I won't betray him."

"I can find out," said Harold.

"But you won't, because I forbid it." She took his hand and pressed it to her cheek. "I know you tried, Stenson. I thought if I could just get rid of the drugs, I could save more of these children. But the harder I tried, the worse it seemed to get."

She looked up at Simon and held out her wrists again. "I would like to speak to an advocate."

"No," said Simon. "No advocate."

"What the hells, Buckley?" Harold's face flushed with anger.

"I won't subject the Force or the Royal family to the circus a detention and trial would bring on," said Simon. "Don't mistake me, Princess. I'd like nothing better than to put you in irons and parade you into Wycliffe House. But we're going to be facing a gang war the likes of which this city hasn't seen in a generation. The Force will need every available Keeper on the street. We can't afford to be distracted by a bunch of newsies hanging around looking to dig up the latest dirt on you."

"What choice do you have?" asked Harold. "You've already said you won't look the other way. What do you want from her?"

"She will quietly abdicate her office. Tonight. The King will need to be told the real reason why, but there won't be any formal charges. She will leave the Commonwealth by morning. After that, the Palace can wait a few days, then spin this any way His Majesty chooses."

"Leave? But where shall I go? How shall I live?" Rebeka's composure slipped for the first time.

"I'll be with you, Highness," said Harold. "I will look after you."

"No!" Liam stepped between them and faced Harold. "I will. That is, if you'll have me, Rebeka."

"You've done enough." Harold growled. "But for you, she'd still be safe."

"That's not true, Stenson. I'd be so much worse." She stood and took Liam's hand. "If not for Liam, I might have hurt someone else, maybe someone I love. Maybe even you or Father. I'd already lost control of the magic. Liam showed me I could be the master, not the slave to the Fire."

"You can still control it." Liam took her other hand in

ABOUT THE AUTHOR:

Bruce Davis is a Mesa AZ based general and trauma surgeon. He finished medical school at the University of Illinois College of Medicine in Chicago way back in the 1970's and did his surgical residency at Bethesda Naval Hospital. After 14 years on active duty that included overseas duty with the Seabees, time on large gray boats and a tour with the Marines during the First Gulf War, he went into private practice near Phoenix. He is part of that dying breed of dinosaurs, the solo general surgeon.

He is also a writer of science fiction and fantasy novels. His independently published works include the YA novel *Queen Mab Courtesy*, and his military science fiction novel *That Which Is Human*. His nonfiction memoir, *Dancing in the Operating Room*, is a glimpse into the life and training of a Trauma Surgeon. *Glowgems for Profit* and *Thieves Profit* are parts of a continuing series of stand-alone novels about Zach Mbele, former Republic of Mars commando and captain of the fast freighter, Profit. They and his recent novel, *Platinum Magic* (his first foray into the world of fantasy) are published by Brick Cave Media. *Gold Magic* is the second book in his *Magic Law* series set in a surprising modern world, like our own, only different.

Made in the USA
Middletown, DE
14 March 2023